TODD SWEENEY

The Fiend of Fleet High

ALSO BY DAVID PRATT

Wallaçonia (novel)
Looking After Joey (novel)
My Movie (stories)
Bob the Book (novel)

Todd Sweeney
The Fiend of Fleet High

A Thriller

David Pratt

Ann Arbor, Michigan

Hosta Press
Ann Arbor, Michigan, U.S.A.
hostapress@gmail.com
www.hostapress.com

First U.S. Edition, 2019
Printed in the United States of America

ISBN: 978-1-7329414-0-3

Library of Congress Control Number: 2018914136

Cover design, photography, and calligraphy: Nicholas Williams
Model: John Corser
Interior design: Kelly Smith

*This story is for all the women who
hold stuff together, century after century*

AUTHOR'S NOTE

The legend of Sweeney Todd was first written down by Thomas Peckett Prest in his "penny dreadful" *The String of Pearls, or, The Fiend of Fleet Stree*t (1846). George Dibdin Pitt adapted *String of Pearls* for the London stage in 1847. Pitt's play became the source for Christopher Bond's *Sweeney Todd, the Demon Barber of Fleet Street* (1973), which in turn became the source for the popular musical and film thereof. (All Sweeneys before mine have been barbers.) And there have been many other *Sweeneys*, including theatrical versions in 1865 and 1962, a 1959 ballet, two silent films in the 1920s, a talkie in 1936, a rock musical for high schoolers called *The Sweeney Todd Shock 'n Roll Show*, and a 2006 BBC movie. The theory that Sweeney Todd was a real person, active in London or Paris around 1800, has never been proven. Or disproven.

—DP

TODD SWEENEY

The Fiend of Fleet High

CHAPTER ONE

*A mother and a son reunited—A deeply affecting scene
of maternal and filial affection—Yet dark forebodings
impinge upon the tender scene*

"Squeers? Came after you?" Todd stiffened. "Oh, Mother!
Oh, I'll get him! I promise you, I will—"

"Shush, Todd!" Mrs. Sweeney patted her son's broad
back—the son returned at last, after a lonely and desperate
year. "He never actually *did* anything!"

"To think of that *thing* even coming near you!" Todd's
eyes filled with tears. "'Guidance counselor!' I'd like to
guide his—"

"Todd!"

"I'm sorry, Mother." He slumped. His sweater hung
loose. She could see how much weight he had lost. Yet he
had gained muscle. "I should have been here to protect
you. Mom, I'm so sorry!" His shoulders began to shake; he
covered his tear-stained eyes with his large hand. "I'll get
him!" he snarled. "I'll get that bastard—"

"Sh-sh-sh," his mother said, rocking him. "It wasn't your
fault. We'll just be grateful you're home from"—she made a
face—"'*boot camp.*' And that they agreed I could send you
to that private place. It was maybe a little more civilized."

3

"Only 'cause you used your social-work connections and paid for it yourself!" Todd cried. "You had to sell all our—" His handsome, stricken face looked around their once cozy living room, stripped of its old, familiar heirlooms. "Mom, I swear I'll make it up to you."

She took his face in her hands, felt the rough stubble, and looked into his dark, vulnerable eyes. Her own eyes, deeply set in her sweet face, more lined than a year ago, pled with him. "Darling, there is nothing to make up. We know Squeers lied. You never should have been sent away. You're an honors student and just a pillar of Fleet High! But once you *were* sent away and Squeers started coming around, we knew why he did it!"

"Mom: did he ever actually touch you?"

"Todd, *please.*"

"He did, didn't he? I'll get that—"

"Todd! We're not going to 'get' anyone. It's over. We're going back to how things were." Her fingers played absently with a hole in her sweater, trying to patch it over with the loose strands of yarn. "You'll finish school with all A's and go to college, and it will be as though Squeers never existed."

Tears glistened in Todd's eyes. He saw what the ordeal had done to his mother. Her hair grayer, the spark in her eyes dimmed. She would never be the same. It reminded him that someday she would die, just as his father had, and he couldn't bear it. "Mom?" His voice trembled. "You know, before Dad died, he held me in his arms." He put his arms around his mother. "And he made me promise to take care of you." Mrs. Sweeney looked down, her sunken cheeks soft in the lamplight. "But we can never go back to how it was. I trust no one now!"

"Todd," she sighed, resting her face against the top of his head, "you're such a good son. Your father would be proud of how you handled all this adversity and how you take care of me." Her chin quivered. "I put flowers on his grave

4

and I said, 'Richard, don't you worry. We're bearing up, Todd and I.'" Her voice broke. "And if it's winter, I say, 'Stay warm, Richard.' It's silly, but I still like to worry about him."

Todd quietly cried.

"He loved you so much. From the second he saw you. You were the most special thing."

"I love you, too, Mom. Always."

"And you are as pure and beautiful as you were the second we laid eyes on you, Todd Sweeney. And now, I want you to get some sleep! Senior year starts next week!"

"I think I'm going to take a little walk, Mom. You know, look at the old neighborhood. If I go to bed now, I'll just worry."

"Well, don't be too long."

"I won't." He rose and put on his jacket. "I promise."

She stood and came to him and fixed his collar. "And don't you worry. I told Squeers I had no interest, and he went away. Now, we'll just take care of each other."

"That's right, Mom." But he sounded distant.

She went up on tiptoes to kiss him. "Whatever's making you angry, Todd, just forget about it. Pray for it to go away, and it will. You have a nice walk now. I'll listen for you to come in."

"Sure, Mom."

After a last hug and kiss, he stepped out into the night air. From their broad, deep porch he listened to the creep-creep of crickets. Beneath his feet the boards, paint peeling, suddenly cried. Petunias overflowed baskets. Soon they'd be gone, and she'd put out bittersweet. As though either could really help. He stepped to the edge.

Then down he dove into the stillness and silence. From the auras of street lamps he stole looks into the shadows. What waited there? And what move was it about to make?

CHAPTER TWO

Childhood friends, together once more—A boy pines for his lost love—An emotional scene between father and son, during which our hero displays great resolve

A shadow behind a curtain. A lone figure at a kitchen sink. Out front of one dark house: "Home of a Fleet High Eagle." They had signs for honor students, too, but whenever he had asked, they were somehow out.

A cat stole out of dark weeds—like Ashford Squeers, Fleet High's guidance counselor, come creeping, slithering after his mother. What did he say? What did he *do? Had* he touched her? *Had he?* It made Todd crazy.

After a year at Big Adventure Boys' Boot Camp, Todd knew what people would do. They told you to be good and to obey. So you *were* good and you *did* obey, but still they mowed you down. They lied, others went along, and the liars got promoted and won awards, while the silent, exhausted thousands just slept through it all.

A cry from the dark streets. The world mourning its fate. No, it was a person. A familiar voice. He stumbled forward. Was it behind this bent gate that would never swing again? Under that scraggly hedge? "Where are you?" he begged. The voice cried on.

Then, on a stump in an empty lot, shivering, shoulders heaving, wiping tears, a boy huddled in a too-big long-sleeve T-shirt and baggy brown pants. The boy's hands were drawn up, and he clutched the cloth of his sleeves in his fists. "Toby!"

"No, it's no one," the boy moaned. Then he looked up. "Oh, my God! Todd? Is it you?"

Todd ran and threw his arms around the sobbing boy. As always, delicate, beautiful Toby fit into Todd's enveloping arms, his slender face nuzzling Todd's chest. "Tobes, what's wrong?" The boy's unruly curls were warm and sweet-smelling. Todd kissed the top of his head.

"Everything's wrong!" Toby bawled. "It'll never be right again."

"It will, Tobes, I promise." The weight of the boy against him made him feel strong. Like a protector. His chest went watery and he could feel his heartbeat. "Tobes, is it Anthony?"

"Yes! They sent him away!" Toby wailed. "The only guy I ever loved!"

"Who? Who sent him where?"

"Squeers! He got together with Anthony's parents, and they put him in the Bending Sheep!"

"The gay conversion place?" Todd asked. He hugged Toby hard to him and stroked his hair.

"It's *miles* from here. I'll never see him again. I love him so much, but they're going to mess up his mind, my sweet Anthony, and he'll never be the same!"

"Squeers!" Todd snarled. "God damn him!"

"It's worse'n that," said Toby. "He wants to send me, too. To a different place. He convinced my parents. I won't survive, Todd. I decided, I'm keeping pills in my room, enough to, well, you know, if they—"

"No, Toby!"

"If they come for me, I'll take them!"

"You are not going to do that, Toby!" Todd clutched the

boy. "You're coming home with me now, like old times, and we're going to figure this out." He rocked Toby. "We are not giving up, and we are not letting garbage like Squeers control our lives!"

"What choice do we have?"

"There is always a choice, Toby."

"I missed you so much!" Toby sniffled.

"I missed you, too!" said Todd. "No one to help me with my math, no one to make me watch obscure movies or drive around with me at night!"

"Boot camp was hell, huh?" Toby said. "And here I am carrying on."

"You have every right!" Todd said. "We're gonna fix it!"

"The worst," Toby said, "must've been knowing the so-called 'guidance counselor' got you put there for no reason."

"Oh, he had reasons," Todd said.

"Like what?"

"Like, never mind. He thinks I don't know. He thinks I can't get back at him. He's gonna find out differently."

"He threatened to tell my parents I'm gay," Toby sighed. "His brother-in-law or someone owns the conversion camp where he wants to put me."

"Well, he can't do that!"

"But what am I gonna do?" Toby sobbed. "Take the *millions* I earn from mowing lawns and, like, *sue* him? Anyone can do anything they want!"

"Not with me here!" Todd snapped. "Call and tell your mom you're staying at my house tonight. My mom won't mind."

"They won't let me. Not since you went to reform school. I couldn't even visit you there."

"Tell 'em I got religion when I was there. Say we're gonna have Bible study. Go on!"

Slowly Toby pulled out his phone and called his mother. "M-Mom?" he said. "Yeah, um, I've got great news. Well,

9

I think there's another lamb in the fold. T-Todd came home, from re-f-form school? And he saw the light." Todd grinned. "We were just discussing, you know, the Bible." Todd took the phone. "Mrs. Ragg? God bless you, ma'am. I cannot tell you what I have been through, ma'am, and what a relief it has been for my soul to be saved."

Soon Todd convinced Toby's mother that a Bible-study sleepover was the best idea in the world. She actually thanked him. Then Toby took the phone to receive the usual admonitions. After he hung up, he slumped.

"Whatsa matter?" Todd asked. "It worked!"

"It's still only a matter of time," Toby sighed. "They'll find out, or Squeers will tell them."

Todd thought he should give Toby a pep talk, but he couldn't muster it. He knew what the Raggs were like—what everyone was like!—and how they could all pretty much do any mean, nasty thing they wanted. But Todd steeled himself. He would protect Toby. He would protect his mother.

How, though?

Maybe . . . Nellie! Tomorrow, she would be at the farmers' market, raising money for scholarships. She knew how to handle anything. Plus, she was sweet and really beautiful, with auburn hair, a rosebud of a mouth, and sparkling, flir-tatious eyes. And smart. In ninth grade, while everyone else was reading *The Grapes of Wrath*, she had made him read Hesse's *Beneath the Wheel*. He had, in fact, always sort of wanted to go out with her, but he saw himself as bumbling and ineffectual next to her. He certainly wasn't sure how to protect Toby. Or how to protect his very own mother!

But.

This awful business with Squeers and everyone—this was a mission *made* for beautiful, sweet Nellie Lovett.

His phone buzzed with a text from his mother: "Are you all right?" Todd texted back, "Ran into Toby, can he stay over, his mom says OK?" Mrs. Sweeney: "Really?" Todd assured her he had convinced Mrs. Ragg. "Then you better get back here," the next text said. "Don't want 2B out in the dark." Todd smiled. "2B" was the only abbreviation his mother used, and it took her just as long to type as "to be" did.

"One more stop for me," Todd texted back. "I think you know where." His mother responded with five hearts (the only emoji she used), X's, O's, and "See you soon."

"Where?" Toby asked, peering over Todd's shoulder.

"There's someone I haven't seen yet," Todd said.

"I bet I know. Can I come, too?"

"Not all the way. You can come as far as the river."

They crept from the empty lot, stole past the mall at the west end of town, descended into the knife-like shadow of a concrete wall, and vanished under the railroad bridge. Down East River Avenue, Todd walked on the outside, shielding Toby, but there were few cars this late. Todd could see his young friend's sweet face, the skin so perfectly pale in the glow of street lights. They heard the river babble. Above the trees on the opposite bank, the First Church steeple rose. "Wait for me," Todd said. "And don't fall asleep!"

Toby promised he wouldn't. Todd tousled his hair and stepped away. Then he swung back and gave Toby a kiss on the forehead. He bounded up to the bridge and jogged across, his sneakers making a hollow plunk-plunk. Toby went to the water's edge and hid in the reeds, the liquid cacophony close. A car swooshed overhead. He heard male voices from Biggs's Ice Cream up the road. Loud. Mocking. Engines gunned.

Todd strode up the First Church lawn. Lights illuminated a sign saying Sunday services were at 9:30 and 11:00. Beneath that, "Chicken Supper, Sat. 9/14, 6pm." The church windows were pitch black, the lawn dim, grass and shadows of grass like tiny knives. Beyond, a stone maze. Steles and angels rose against the stars. Crickets chirped a hymn to the forgotten.

Slowly, as Todd walked among them, the stones distinguished themselves, some tall, staking out iron-fenced plots for wealthy families; some, like the one Todd at last approached, low and humble, tributes to ordinary men and women, rarely read or even noticed. He crouched and shined his cell phone down. His heart jolted when he saw:

"George Richard Sweeney, Teacher, Benefactor, Loving Husband and Father." Two dates, forty-eight years apart. A dead geranium his mother had put there in summer, probably for Father's Day, from the two of them, though back then Todd had been toiling under the hot sun at Big Adventure.

He sat on the hard ground, lowered his body across the stone, and hugged it. "Hi, Dad," he said, his voice breaking. "How you doing?" His tears flowed. "Mom says you worry about us. Well, don't, Dad. We miss you, but we're gonna be okay. I wish every day that you'd come back. I probably always will. But we're getting on fine, Mom and me. And I have my kid brother. You remember Toby. You guys said he was your second son. Well, I'm taking care of Toby, and he's taking care of me, just like he was my brother. You'd be proud to have a son like him, Dad, and you'd be proud how I take care of him."

Todd felt the gritty stone against his cheek. "Dad, I wanna be just like you. You helped so many people, and you protected me, and I'm gonna protect Mom and Toby. You'll see, Dad," he said, turning his face to kiss the stone, "you'll see what a good protector I am."

"Todd!" a voice whispered.

Todd rose onto his knees and turned his cell phone toward Toby. "Tobes! I told you to wait!"

"You took so long, I got worried." He looked down at the stone before which Todd sat. "Hey, Mr. Sweeney," he said. "It's good to see you."

Todd caressed the stone. "I'm sure it's good for him to see you, Tobes," he said. "It's good for him to see us together."

"Seriously, though, Todd. Guys come in here and tip the stones over. And at the Jewish cemetery they spray swastikas."

"You're kidding! I mean, we're not the most advanced town, but—" He saw the boy shivering, and he rose. "Worry no more, little bro," he said. He enveloped Toby in his arms again, and Toby clung to him. Todd whispered in his young friend's ear. "I was telling Dad again about how you're like a brother to me. Remember how he used to call you his 'second son'? Mom still does."

"And I called them my second parents. And you *are* my brother, Todd, and I love you."

"I love you, too, Tobes. Hey, we should get going. Don't wanna worry Mom!"

Todd held up his phone screen and together they found their way out of the stone maze and back across the bridge. "Your dad was the best," Toby said. "All the kids he taught and helped. They still say he was the best. And volunteering and all. There was no one he wouldn't help. You and your folks are my heroes, Todd."

"And you're our hero, little brother!" Todd said, and tousled his friend's hair.

They entered the still, silent center of town—thrift shop, bridal shop, insurance agency, dollar store, all dark. The stoplights flashed yellow. Flower baskets swung and vertical banners flapped from streetlights. On the banners, the town's name in block letters. Beneath, in curlicued script, the words "Feel the Charm."

In the warm, dim light of Todd's bedroom, Toby stood in his underpants. Todd tossed him a pair of pajama bottoms. Toby pulled them on and climbed into bed. Todd, in a pair

13

of cut-off sweats, slid in and turned out the light. He raised his arm just as he had hundreds of times over the years, so Toby could snuggle under it. Todd then closed both arms around Toby's thin body. "It's gonna be okay, Tobes," he said. He felt a swelling in his chest. He was free. He was a man again. And men protected the ones they loved. His dad had protected him, and he would protect Toby. Though younger, Toby had done so much for him—helping him with math in elementary school, helping him pass Chemistry and Algebra II at Fleet High, being there when his dad died, always being available for long drives at night with sudden stops at Dairy Queens and IHOPs. "We'll get you through it all," he said. "I'll be right here. I will never leave you."

Toby squirmed himself closer, nuzzling Todd's chest. Todd smiled, thinking how his favorite thing about his body was his chest hair, just like his dad's. The sign that he, too, was strong and capable.

"Tobes?" Todd said.

"Mm?"

"Someday, you know, I'm gonna get married and all. And I'm gonna have a son. And Tobes? I want him to be just like you."

Toby giggled. "Well," he said. "Except for, well, you know."

"No 'except,'" Todd said. "I want him to be *exactly* like you."

"Yeah," said Toby, "just not—"

"Tobias. For the third time. I want my son to be just. Like. You. Exactly. Okay?"

"Okay."

"Good night. I love you, Toby."

"I love you, Todd. Welcome home!"

Snuggled together, the two young men fell asleep.

14

At four a.m., Todd woke with one of the most beautiful feelings he knew. He had an erection, so hard it ached, but he reveled in it. Not that he and Toby would do anything now, tonight. They had played around in the beginning of high school, knowing it would bring them closer to ejaculate together. As they grew, though, they went back to just cuddling. Then came Todd's terrible year away. Now Todd held Toby and reveled in the thought that the ache between his legs meant he was fit for his job as a man. *I'll watch over you,* he thought. *I am strong, and no harm can possibly come to you.*

This thought was so beautiful to him that he promptly, fully, luxuriously ejaculated.

CHAPTER THREE

*Mr. Squeers's vile threats—A callow youth's rage at those
who hold the reins of power—Mrs. Sweeney distraught—
A culinary scene may foreshadow a violent turn of events*

Nellie Lovett, fresh faced, beaming and batting her eyes,
called in a sweet, musical voice, "Empanadas! Fresh, hot
empanadas!" On the town green, the Saturday farmers'
market swirled and buzzed around her. Decent people.
Good food. Straight from—
"This ain't hot!" boomed a voice behind her. She
whipped around.
"Ain't fresh, either!" said another voice.
"That's two dollars, Ryan!" she demanded of the first
boy, who was stuffing his mouth with an apple empanada.
Filling spilled on his Fleet High Eagles T-shirt but he didn't
notice.
"Don't get your knickers in a twist!" Ryan said. His lower
lip hung away from a row of crooked teeth. He hadn't
shaved or, it seemed, washed his hair.
"Or your tits in a wringer," said Taylor, the other boy. He
had acne and no lips. His T-shirt said "I Hate T-Shirts."
Ryan threw two dollars down. "This is terrible!" he said,
shoving the rest in his mouth. "Least it's for a 'good

cause.'" He snorted. "Sendin' immigrants to college who're gonna flunk anyway!" He laughed and the chewed empanada showed. "Here," said Taylor, tossing a single bill on the table. "Give this to some *muchacho* for remedial English. Just don't make me eat one of them things!" Ryan hooted. The two boys loped away.

Nellie breathed deeply and tried to let go of her rage. Ryan had been right about one thing. The empanadas might be reasonably warm and the ingredients sort of fresh, but overall the product was inferior. Bruised, mealy apples and tough chicken were all she could afford. But it was indeed for a good cause: helping Fleet High kids go to the U downstate. And Nellie's mother suffered from eye problems, so Nellie helped with that, too. Her dad had taken a third job, but it still wasn't enough. She took a deep breath. "Empanadas! Fresh, um, empanadas!"

"Hey, it's lovely Nellie Lovett!"

Who was giving her grief now? "Todd Sweeney! Holy guacamole!" She smiled with an adorable twist to her mouth and said more softly, "You're out of the slammer!"

"Yeah, finally!" They hugged. "Can I get a cheese and an apple?"

"You sure?"

"Course I'm sure." He looked at her worried brow. "Hey, why's the weather so cloudy?"

"Ryan Plouf just insulted the goods."

"Where is he?" Todd grinned. "I'll kill him. I'm an 'ex-con' now, anyway."

"And he's a dick, but he's not wrong. I try to make them cheap, but— And people buy just 'cause they feel sorry. When did you get back?"

"Last night. Did you know this stuff that's been going on with Tobes?"

"Like, Anthony being sent to that conversion camp? And Squeers wants to out Toby to his parents and put him into the same kind of place!"

"Isn't that mixing church and state—Squeers putting a kid in gay rehab because of his own beliefs?"

"His cousin or something runs the place. It's mixing capitalism with hey-I'm-a-public-school-employee-in-a-union-so-you-can't-fire-me. Squeers is hideous! Well, I don't have to tell you. A year in Big Adventure! Look at you. Poor thing. How did you stand it?"

"By fantasizing what I'd do to Squeers when I got out. So they really can't fire him?"

"Supposedly behavior problems at Fleet are down. And the church people on the town council love him. 'Scuse me a sec. Empanadas! Fresh empanadas! Speaking of capitalism."

Todd put four dollars on the table and took an apple and a cheese.

"Hideous, right?" Nellie said, wincing, as Todd bit into the cheese.

"Not at all," said Todd. "But there is a high crust-to-filling ratio. Do you have some water?"

"Right here. Crust is cheap. So what fantasies do you have about Squeers?"

Todd swigged and took another bite of empanada. "Catching him in a men's room on his knees?"

"Good one! Probably not far off. 'Scuse me again. Empanadas!" Suddenly she stared at a point just over Todd's right shoulder. Her eyes grew wide.

"What?" said Todd. He turned.

"Sweeney!" said a tall, twisted figure, its face not just weathered or wrinkled, but crushed, like a ball of paper, into a permanent sneer. It came right up to him. "Well? What do you say to your elders, Sweeney?"

"Mr. Squeers," Todd said evenly. He kept his gaze down. He hated to think this looked like deference, when in fact he just couldn't stand to look at the man.

"Mr. Sweeney," said Ashford Squeers. "I believe we will be seeing a lot of one another this year."

19

Todd swallowed. He could feel Nellie standing staunchly at his shoulder. Yes, she always knew what to do.

Squeers leaned in, his face twisted with rage and resentment. His breath stank so Todd nearly gagged, and he hadn't shaved. His stained shirt stretched across his belly, one button about to pop. "You will be reporting to me daily, Sweeney," Squeers growled, "4:00 p.m., sharp. I will be watching your every move, and I will be ready to send you back to juvie like *that!*" He snapped his thick dirty fingers, with their thick, dirty nails, right under Todd's face. His cracked lips parted to reveal yellow teeth with tooth cheese in the crevices. "And if you fail to appear on time, you will take a stroke—no, *two* strokes—of the paddle for every minute you are late." He chuckled, low in his throat. Todd's own throat closed. Not about the paddling. It had happened before. It was the way Squeers somehow got to do anything he wanted. There were specific rules about paddling in their state. Squeers ignored them. Year after year. What you could say to students, what you could do to students, Squeers ignored it all, and all anyone said was, "Well, he's tough." Or, "He doesn't *really* mean anything by it." Some parents even said, "I wish I'd had someone like that setting me straight when I was your age."

Squeers glanced at Nellie.

"As for your *girlfriend* here," he sneered. "I am not contributing one penny to your alleged *scholarship* effort. If the Lord wants a student to go to some fancy university, He will send him. All you're trying to do"—he stuck a filthy finger in Nellie's face—"is send a bunch of immigrant underachievers to do what they aren't meant to do. Just 'cause they're 'Muslim' or 'Hispanic' or some nonsense." He shifted the finger back to Todd. "Monday. Four o'clock. Our first little chat. And if you *are* late, Sweeney, try to be, oh, about fifteen minutes or twenty late. So I can really have some fun! Did I mention you take those strokes bare bottom?" Squeers cackled, releasing puffs of hot stench, turned, and swaggered off.

Todd was left coughing and trembling. He wanted to say, to shout, a hundred things he could not. Then Squeers turned back. He put his stubbled face right up to Todd's. "And Sweeney?" he growled low, so only Todd could hear. "Tell your mamma I said hello." Todd nearly choked. "Tell her I'll be calling soon. With a little invitation. And she better say yes, because the topic of our conversation is going to be your success in school." Squeers poked Todd in the chest. "So if she doesn't say an enthusiastic yes to dear old Squeers, she just might find her precious sonny-boy taken away again!"

Squeers's face collapsed into a grotesque parody of grief. "'To think of that *thing* coming near you!'" he wailed. "'And I wasn't here to protect you. Mother, I'm so sorry!'"

Todd's eyes went wide.

"Yeah, I was listening," Squeers said. "I watch, I listen, and you can't stop me. And neither can Mamma, and neither can poor, dead Daddy in the cemetery. I've already turned that school around from how Daddy ruined it with all his permissive liberal drivel. I even moved into his office. And pretty soon, if your mama just decides to cooperate, I'm going to occupy some other places Daddy used to occupy. And you'll have a *new* daddy. And no 'little brother' to turn to. We're sending him to get the perversion programmed out of him. Ha! See you Monday, Sweeney. And one more little thing."

"What?" Todd asked hoarsely.

"Tell your little friend over there she doesn't have to try so hard with those turnover things. That African refugee kid? Jeez, who can even pronounce his name? He's—"

Todd looked Squeers in the eye and articulated every syllable: "Bamedele Cetshwayo." Across the green, as though from another lifetime, he heard kids playing.

"Yeah," Squeers snapped. "'Mr. Rama-lama-ding-dong.'

21

I don't like him in my school. Taking up space that could go to a real American. He'll be gone by Christmas, Sweeney. Wait and see." And with that Squeers straightened up, turned on his heel, and strode away.

Todd slowly turned to Nellie, his eyes wide. She gripped his arm. "My God!" she whispered. "What did he say?"

After a pause, in a low, cold voice, Todd said, "A lotta stuff. He said a lotta stuff."

"I guess!" Nellie said, "You look awful. *He* looked awful. I'd offer you another empanada but it'd make you worse. What's this about paddling, anyway? Aren't there rules about that? Doesn't there have to be a witness, and you can only—"

Breathing through his mouth, Todd said, "There's rules about a lot of stuff." He looked after Squeers. "But rules don't stop some people. There's 'religious' people on the school board who say the rules are wrong. They look the other way. The rest of the board's rich people, like Tawsey Speedwell? Craft's dad? Squeers is nice as pie to them. So they've got his back. No pun intended. You know, he supposedly makes guys strip and grab their ankles." He took a big, gulping breath. "No one wants to 'squeal.' No one wants to be the guy on the front page of the town paper—if it even gets that far—admitting he's 'not man enough to take it.' Y'know, they show it off, in the locker room. 'Look, guys. The Mark of Squeers!' Like a contest, who got it worse."

Nellie scoffed. "Men!" she said. And she winked at Todd and he suddenly felt weak in his knees in a much more pleasurable way.

Suddenly a voice called, "Oh, my goodness! Is that Todd?"

Todd and Nellie turned. "Mrs. Bishop!" they said in unison.

The Fleet High math teacher, with her sweet smile and her neat, closely trimmed cap of gray hair, came trotting toward them. She wore a crocheted top, a #MeToo button pinned to it, tan slacks, and walking shoes. She held up four bills. "One cheese, one chicken, please!" she sang, in such a sure voice that suddenly it seemed everything would be all right again.

Nellie assembled the empanadas. "You're such a loyal customer, Mrs. Bishop," she marveled.

"Well, they're awfully good," said Mrs. Bishop. "And for a good cause, of course. How are your mother's eyes, Nellie?"

"Oh, she gets along. But their insurance isn't very good. My dad works as hard as he can, though. Three jobs now."

"Oh, dear! Well, tell them I'll visit soon. Now, Todd!" She gave him a hug. "I'd heard you were back! It's so good to see you!"

"Thank you, Mrs. Bishop," Todd said. "I wish everyone was so happy to see me."

She frowned. "Who isn't?" she demanded.

"Well—"

"Squeers? I saw him over here a minute ago."

"He's still not too happy with me."

Mrs. Bishop drew herself up. "Persons like Mr. Squeers," she opined, "have no business in the educational system. I don't know how he does it, getting reported and weaseling out every time. It burns me up! But you won't let that ogre stop you, Todd. You'll bounce back and do great things! Won't he, Nellie?"

"He certainly will," Nellie said. "Here's your order, Mrs. B."

"Thank you, dear! And Todd, I will see you in AP Calculus next week!"

"I dunno, Mrs. B.," Todd stammered. "Where I was, you know, the classes weren't so good. I think I lost some ground."

"No worry," Mrs. Bishop sang. "We'll get Bammy Cetshwayo to tutor you. Always accept a challenge. That's what I say!"

"Yeah," Todd said. His eyes strayed off to where Squeers had disappeared in the crowd. "Maybe you're right. Always accept a challenge."

"Of course I'm right!" said Mrs. Bishop. "Toodle-oo, everyone." Then she, too, was gone.

"She is so lovely," Nellie sighed.

"Everybody should be like that," said Todd. "But her being lovely doesn't change anything. Squeers—*he* changes things. He could send me away. Wreck Toby's life. Now he says he's going after Bammy Cetshwayo. Speaking of."

"Let him try!" Nellie said. "Bammy gets straight A's."

"If anyone can, Squeers can," Todd sneered. "Nellie, what am I gonna do about Tobes?"

"Maybe you have to step back, you know?"

"Not give up!"

"No, *step back*."

"Nellie, a man protects. That's what a man does. That's what my dad did!"

"But even the biggest, strongest man can't fix everything. Even your dad couldn't. Not every time." She touched his forearm.

"If anything happens to Toby—" Todd's lip trembled. A tear crept into his eye and Nellie smiled and embraced him. "If they try to do the slightest thing to him, this town's gonna see something like it ain't seen in all its days."

"Easy, Todd," Nellie said. "Let's just wait and—"

"Easy?" Todd spat, looking around the farmers' market, as though potential evil lurked in every stall. "It definitely won't be easy."

Todd spent the rest of the morning on the green, helping Nellie and catching up with friends. Squeers had left. Everyone else was happy to see Todd.

He headed home as shadows began to fall. But wait. No light in the kitchen. He hurried in through the back door. His mother wasn't there. There were no pots on the stove.

24

He went to the fridge to see what he should take out. Then he heard crying.

Up the stairs he followed the pathetic sound, and down the upstairs hall. "Mom? What is it?"

When he finally stood before her she looked up, her face wet, her eyes full of tears. "*He* was here!" she wailed. "That's what it is! And he said terrible, awful things. About us. About your father. Somehow he *listens* to us, Todd. He creeps around and hears things we say—and *he knows*! What are we going to do, Todd? What ever are we going to do?"

After a pause, Todd said, "I have an appointment with him Monday, Mom. I'll talk to him. Everything is going to be fine. I'm going to make dinner now, and we're going to have a nice evening. We'll clear everything up on Monday."

His mother studied his face. "All right," she said. "I'll take your word for it. But Todd, the way you look, it's worrying me. Just promise me you won't do anything rash."

"No," Todd said quietly, not meeting her eyes. "Of course not." He kissed her and left.

He descended to the kitchen. He opened the refrigerator and took vegetables from the crisper. He peeled an onion, took a knife from a drawer, and with one stroke cut it in half. He brought the knife down so hard that half the onion flew across the room and knocked a teacup from the dish drainer. It shattered on the floor.

CHAPTER FOUR

A heartfelt scene of epistolary desperation—
The clock ticks—A young migrant's life devastated
by Squeers—A meeting becomes a showdown

Alone after midnight Toby sat in dim light and wrote on a pad with Wonder Woman in the corner. He began with a white lie, the one he always told, or the letter would never get to Anthony. "My dearest brother Anthony," he began, pausing to remember with sweet sorrow Anthony's soft, honey-blond hair and bashful smile.

"You don't know how much I long for you. I see your face in front of me every minute of the day. To think of a world without you destroys me. I hope you think of me, too, and how much I love you. I hope you know you are beautiful and good and will triumph in the end.

"I know you can't write or call. But I imagine what you would say if you could, how much love you have for me and how much you want to be with me. I pray I will be. I know God hears. I just know He wants us to be together again."

And then Toby signed off as he always did, with another lie to get the letter past the authorities at the Bending Sheep. "Love, your sister, Cordelia."

He put the letter in an envelope, addressed it, and stamped it, and then, as tears streamed down his face, he took another sheet of paper, thick, creamy paper he had bought at the stationery store at the mall, and began madly to write the letter he really wanted to write, the one he could never send, telling Anthony of the kisses he would cover him with, telling him how their naked bodies would feel together, telling him how he would be devoted forever, would run away with him, live with him, hold him, cherish him, and wear his ring for the rest of time, if only they could escape the terrible people who wanted to twist their minds and ruin their lives. "And if we can't," Toby concluded, scrawling on paper now wet with tears, a heartbreaking cry streaming from his contorted mouth, then contained, "I don't want to go on living. I refuse to live if I can't be with you!"

And then he collapsed, sobbing, on the letter that would never be sent, that would never be read by anyone in all the world.

Monday afternoon, Todd watched the numerals on his cell phone change:

4:00 . . . 4:01 . . . 4:02 . . .

His calendar had popped up "Meeting w Squeers." He touched the X in the corner and went back to reading *Tess of the d'Urbervilles*. (Nellie: "They should really have us read *Jude the Obscure*. Where they slaughter the pig? *That's* literature!") Todd smiled.

4:10 . . . 4:11 . . . 4:12 . . .

At 4:20 he went to the cafeteria for a mocha and a nut bar. Manuel Martinez sat in a corner, his head on his folded arms, sobbing. "Manny?" Todd said. "*Vete!*" Manuel wailed. "*Vete, vete!*" He waved an arm at Todd without looking up. Slowly Todd retreated. Who had done what to poor Manny, arrived from Mexico only a few months ago?

He returned to the library and checked Facebook. Then he sent some texts to friends, including Toby, who was studying Physics and, as usual, worrying.

"Deep breath, Tobes," Todd texted. "Everything will work out. I promise."

At 4:45 he stood and paced, but with a spring in his step. He breathed deeply, preparing.

4:46 . . . 4:47 . . . 4:48 . . .

At 4:51, a flurry of badly spelled texts from Toby. Added up they said, "oMG ju sthear d mom& dad mtg w squeers tmrwo what m ik fonna do?"

Todd regarded the string of texts and sighed before texting back, "Ur gonna relax and let me handle this."

"Byt how?" Toby texted back.

"You don't have to know that," Todd responded. "Just trust me."

Toby did not respond.

4:55.

Todd assembled his books and backpack. He shouldered the pack and strolled out the library door. He maintained his measured pace as he turned into the hallway leading to the administrative offices.

4:57.

From where he stood he couldn't see if anyone was in. But he knew Squeers had waited. The promise of beating a student could keep him there all night.

4:58.

Todd took deep, even breaths and slowly smiled.

4:59.

His hand on the door. Breathe. Wait.

5:00.

Go!

In one motion he swung the door open, ducked around the corner, and stood in what, a lifetime ago, it seemed, had been his father's office. Now it belonged to the man standing, sneering, arms folded, behind a desk with fake wood grain. Ashford Squeers. Gone were Todd's father's portraits of Dr. King and Jane Addams. They had not even been returned to the family. Squeers, or someone, had put up paintings of plaintive, big-eyed kids holding bouquets of flowers. Gone was the green banker's lamp. Squeers stood in cold, fluorescent light. He did not look quite so confident as Todd had thought he would. He seemed taken aback by the suddenness of Todd's appearance, and by the lack of contrition Todd made more than apparent. Squeers leaned forward and with a snarl said, "Sweeney. I assume we are aware what time it is."

"Yessir," Todd said.

A grin wrenched Squeers's lips. He held up one stiff, grimy finger. "One hour," he said, and chuckled. "One hour late, Mr. Sweeney."

"Yes," Todd said. "One hour."

"Sixty minutes!" Squeers chuckled. "Tell me, Sweeney, what is sixty times two?"

"One hundred and twenty, sir."

"Don't think you can fool me with your devil-may-care attitude, Sweeney. You will have your punishment. In a few minutes you will be begging for it to end. *And it will not.*"

"I don't expect it to, sir," Todd said, shifting his backpack. He glanced at the rack full of paddles Squeers had had installed on the wall. Todd felt a tear come, thinking how his dad would never, ever have done such things.

"But first," said Squeers, "I thought you might like to hear an update on your little friend, Tobias Ragg."

"What update?" Todd didn't know about this. Toby hadn't texted back. What—? He tried to keep his composure.

"I see," said Squeers. "Not so devil-may-care now, eh? I am meeting with young Ragg's parents tomorrow. I have some information that they will be very interested in—"

"Speaking of visits," Todd said, his voice hoarse and low, "did you visit my mother last Saturday?"

"What?" Squeers barked. "I'm telling you—"

"Did you. Visit. My mother. On Saturday?" Todd asked again.

"What business is it of yours?" Squeers sneered.

"It is always my business, sir," Todd said, "when some reeking, vicious piece of garbage comes sneaking around *my* house and disturbs *my* mother. Now, I am not saying," he continued, "that any particular reeking, rotten, festering piece of garbage did that. But if a reeking, rotten, festering piece of garbage *did* do that, I would tell him that he had better stop right now, or I would make him very, very sorry."

Squeers moved around his desk, eyes on Todd. "Would you, now?" he rasped. Todd could smell on his breath a foul scent, part cafeteria food, part liquor. Tuna Yum-Yum and Night Train.

"Yes, sir, I would," Todd said.

"If I were you," Squeers replied, "I would spend less time worrying about Mommy, and more time planning how you're going to manage walking for the rest of the week." Squeers grabbed a stout oak paddle from the rack on the wall. The muscles in his forearm flexed. The paddle was a half inch thick with holes in it.

"We shall root out the evil in Mr. Ragg. In the old days they beat this sissy behavior out of you. Just as I am going to beat the arrogance out of you." He held the paddle up in Todd's face. "It's all warmed up," he grinned. "It got a good workout on Manny Mexican's backside just now. You shoulda seen him, right where you're standing, begging. Tears running down his face. I told him, 'In America, men face up to their punishment. You don't like it, you go back to Fagapulco!' In my day, you went mincing around like Manny or like your little friend Ragg, you went to the woodshed and came back a red-blooded American male, or else. What we have in store for Mr. Ragg is more *nuanced* but equally effective. By this time tomorrow your friend will be on a bus to a place I will not disclose. He will be shown the way of the Lord. He will be shown electrodes. And he will come back as manly as I am. What do you think of that, Sweeney?"

Todd's jaw worked and a vein in his neck throbbed.

"Mute, eh, Sweeney? Of course. There is nothing you can say. Just pray your friend gets the message. He will stay in that facility as long as it takes. If he insists on following the way of Satan, you may never see the little mincing sissy again. Now, Sweeney, you are going to strip and assume the position, and you are going to begin your descent into hell on earth."

"No, sir," Todd said. "I am not going to do that."

For a second Squeers looked confounded. Then he shook with rage, for, in the space of that second, Todd had snatched the paddle and he held it upright between them. His knuckles were white.

"Now, lad," Squeers growled, "you don't want to get in any more trouble." He held out his hand. "You're just overexcited." Todd chewed his lip and clutched the paddle. "First week of classes. Back from reform school." Squeers twisted his leathern face into what was meant to be a smile. "Why don't we forget what just happened? Why don't you just hand me that paddle."

Todd narrowed his eyes and shook his head. Squeers took a step toward him. He took a step back. Squeers's voice switched to a higher register, as though he were speaking to a pet. "Tell you what," he said liltingly, "we'll just cut those one hundred and twenty swats in half. Heh-heh. That's what we'll do. That's an awful big break, *Todd*. We'll be done in, oh, not even ten minutes. Then we can shake hands, and you go on your way." Then Squeers frowned. "But, if you continue to hang onto school property like that, if you continue to disobey my direct order, well, then, I might have to, I don't know, call the police, maybe. And gosh darn it, Todd, I don't want to do that. Because, as you and I both know, it wouldn't go very well. Because you have a record."

"Thanks to you!"

"Well, I don't know anything about that. Todd, why don't you just hand me the paddle, we'll take care of our sixty swats in no time, we'll leave your momma out of this, and there won't be any police coming after you."

Squeers closed his hand almost tenderly around the upright paddle. Todd fixed Squeers with a stare. In his head he was calculating. Police. His record. But he had to save Toby. He had to protect his mother. For that he might go to prison anyway.

"Just give me the paddle, and everything will be fine," Squeers cooed. Gently he tugged the paddle from Todd's loosening fist. "That's right," Squeers sighed. "That's a good boy."

And now Squeers had the paddle in his hands.

CHAPTER FIVE

*The kindness of a pure and guileless daughter toward
her long-suffering parents—Terrified texts intervene—
Drawn into a web of violence and deceit, our heroine
displays advanced problem-solving skills—A seemingly
upright soul helps enable the dark and deadly scheme*

"Here you go, Mom," Nellie said, placing a plate of steaming rice, mushrooms, and vegetables in front of her mother.

"Thank you, sweetheart," said Mrs. Lovett. "It smells divine! Nellie, you're so good to me!"

"Mom, I love you!" Nellie said, embracing her mother. She could not help but notice that, while her mother appreciated the aroma of dinner, she was having a hard time seeing it. "I love you both." Her voice broke. "I'm going to serve out a plate for Dad and put it in the microwave."

"Yes, he'll be home around midnight."

"By the way, did I tell you Mrs. Bishop is coming to visit you?"

In her pocket, Nellie's phone buzzed. She pulled it out and looked.

"Am @ school need u RIGHT NOW."

Under her breath she sighed, "Oh, for Heaven's sake!"

She went to get her own plate and then joined her mother. The phone buzzed again: "Nells where r u?"

"Mom, I'm sorry, I have to get this," Nellie said. She put down her own plate and texted, "What?" She did not have the first forkful of vegetables in her mouth before the phone buzzed yet again. "Never mind just pls come 2 admin ofc now!!!!!!!!"

"Mom, I am so sorry," Nellie said.

"It's all right, dear."

"It's just I think there may be some kind of emergency—"

"Oh, dear!"

"—and I should check on it. Todd might be in trouble. I just have to drive over to school."

"Of course," said Mrs. Lovett. "Todd's a nice boy. We don't want him in any trouble."

"And I'll come right back. Promise. We'll watch something together."

"Oh, that will be fun! That's what I look forward to!"

"I know, Mom." Nellie kissed her, gobbled one more mouthful of dinner, and ran out the back door.

Nellie surveyed the walls and floor of Ashford Squeers's office, her eyes wide, her face pale and still in the fluorescent glare. She held Todd's hand tight. "Well!" she said breathlessly. "To quote Lady Macbeth, 'Who would have thought the old man to have had so much blood in him.'"

"Whoa," Todd said. He surveyed the floor and walls. "Yeah. Um. Yeah. Whoa."

Nellie took a deep breath. "Okey-dokey, then," she said. She massaged Todd's hand. "Number one thing is not to panic. Nothing is ever as bad as it looks. No, scratch that. This is probably way worse than it looks."

"He said terrible, terrible things, Nells," Todd moaned. "It wasn't threatening just to me. It was Tobes and my mom and—"

36

Nellie lay a hand on his shoulder. "No no no, sweetie," she said.

Todd took her hand and held it to his face. "And my dad's office!" he bawled suddenly, tears flowing. "This was my dad's office, and now . . . this *thing!*"

"Of course, of course," Nellie said soothingly. "Your choice of, um, victim was totally fine. He's a very bad guy. Was, I mean. That part is just hunky-dory."

"Well what, then?" said Todd, gazing down at Squeers's twisted, motionless form.

Nellie stepped closer to Squeers's body, its head a dark purple paste of blood, brains, and bone. "Well, for starters, and I'm just being factual here, it *is* a crime. But I understand why you did it. I mean, to me you are not a criminal."

"Aw, Nells," Todd said, and they hugged.

In the middle she said, "Um, do you mind if we, like, close the eyes?" She looked at him.

He looked at her.

Finally he knelt and did it, then fell back, shuddering.

"And we will fix it," she said, helping him up. "But, and please don't take this the wrong way." She held his hand to her cheek. "I would just offer some advice, like, so you won't make the same mistake next time."

"What mistake?"

"I know you didn't have a lot of time to think about this," she said sympathetically, "but you really don't want to whack someone in their place of business."

"Why not?"

"Because then, sweetheart, you're not in control of anything. We've got"—she glanced at the clock—"maybe twenty minutes till security comes back. So either we have to turn out the lights and hide and hope they don't come in, or we have to clean up and get him out of here. And I doubt," she said, looking around at the walls, "that we can clean up this blood spatter in twenty minutes. Plus, there's the carpet." She bent down and examined the carpet and the corpse more closely. "Wow, you really did a number on him."

Voice quivering, Todd snarled, "I bladed him! Like, about ten or twelve times."

"You whatted him?"

"Hit him with the edge of the paddle. In the center of his skull. Twelve times." He sounded sadder now.

"You mentioned."

"I think he was dead after the first six or so. The rest were kind of like for me. Is this weird? I'm kinda stoked."

"That's nice," Nellie said. "But it kind of made the room that much messier. Oh, now, see? You're taking this as criticism again. Give me the paddle." Todd held it out to her. Holding the very end of it between thumb and forefinger and making a face, she dropped it into her bag. "I liked this bag," she mused.

"Sorry," Todd said. "I guess I should have googled 'how to kill your guidance counselor' first?"

Nellie sighed. "I'm just saying, look, duct tape, right there. You could have bound him up and then called and we could have had a nice, calm conversation about how to dispose of him. We would have had *options*. Where *is* security, by the way?"

"They went by right before you got here. I turned out the lights. Everybody was happy."

"Okay, so, they have to go around the gym, the bleachers, then back here. So we have some time. Go down to the custodians' closet and see what they've got in the way of carpet cleaner. And four really big plastic bags."

"What does carpet cleaner look like?"

"Usually it's in a container marked 'carpet cleaner,' okay? Go! And find plastic gloves and put them on before you touch anything. And a brush. A stiff one."

Todd, looking silly but kind of adorable, she thought, in bright blue gloves, brought back the carpet cleaner and plastic bags. They sprayed it on the rug and rubbed it in.

"Now we pray," Nellie muttered. "At least it might fade to, like, pink. Okay, unroll the bags. Put his head in first. I don't want to look at that face anymore. What set you off, by the way? You've hated him forever. Why tonight?"

Todd explained about Toby, but he couldn't bring himself to tell Nellie how Squeers had threatened his mother.

"Oh, my God. Disgusting! It sounds like you got him just in time. Give me the gloves."

But now Todd was looking down at Squeers with a peculiar, horrified look, like he would cry or throw up.

"What, sweetie?" Nellie asked softly.

"I just . . . I just never saw . . . before . . . you know, a body." He swallowed. He had gone entirely white. "I mean, I did that. I hated him so much. I had to. But now I look, and . . . and I . . ."

". . . eliminated a very bad, very sick man," Nellie said, "who did very bad, very sick things. Look at me, Todd. In the eye. This is a good thing. This helps innocent, oppressed individuals who would have no other recourse *in the entire world*, because certain people never have any recourse. You may, in fact, have saved lives. Think about that. Are you thinking? Good. Now: gloves."

Todd's shoulders relaxed. He took a deep breath and handed over the gloves. Nellie put them on and went to Squeers's computer keyboard.

"What are you doing?"

"His email's open. I'm sending a message that he's taking a sick day tomorrow. When we leave, we lock the door, and hopefully no one looks in here till maybe Wednesday." She typed and hit "send." Then she bent close to the screen again and clicked around some more.

"Now what?" said Todd.

"Uh-oh!" She made one last mouse-click and turned away.

"What?"

"Nothing. He's just got some pictures in there."

39

"Of guys?"

"Get the brush. Yes. Of guys."

"Always the religious types, isn't it? Anyone we know?"

"Todd! I didn't want to look. I don't want to know. Maybe I saw someone who graduated. A while ago. Nothing else. Okay, carpet cleaner's dry. Brush it away and see what we've got. I'm going to finish wrapping him up. Brush harder. How's it look?" She swung Squeers's feet around and tried to bag them.

"You can still see it."

"Well, like I say, we hope no one comes looking for a few days."

"What about his family?"

"He's divorced. The wife and kids are kinda far, I think." Her eyes went to a framed photo on Squeers's desk. Todd's gaze followed. Quickly she placed the photo face down. "You may have done them a favor," she said. Their eyes met for a long moment. "Really. Think about what he might be doing to them. Hand me the duct tape."

In the end they put together a nice, tidy package. Todd put the gloves on again and straightened the office. Nellie reminded him to log out of the computer. "Now turn out the lights," she said, "and let's go."

"Where are we going to put him?"

"Out by Massauga Wetlands. I know a place."

"You know everything."

"I humbly admit it. Now help me lift."

They closed Squeers's door behind them and half-carried, half-dragged their plastic-wrapped victim out to the door of the administrative suite.

"Whoa! Whoa!" Todd said. "What about cameras?"

"Tsk tsk," Nellie said. "You haven't been keeping up with local news!"

"Like what?"

"Last big budget meeting. It was either security cameras or new football equipment. Guess what won?" She reached to open the door to the corridor. "So, we still only have 'em in front. We're taking him out the back. Uh-oh."

"Uh-oh," Todd echoed. "Um, what?"

"This door doesn't lock automatically."

"He must have a key."

"There's no time to open this up again," Nellie said. "Besides, I sort of patted him down, and I didn't feel anything."

"Then the keys are in his office."

"Which is locked. Maybe security will think it's an oversight and just lock it and think nothing of it."

"Until the cops question them—"

They said together, "On Wednesday." Nellie sighed. "See why you never, *ever* whack anyone in their workplace?"

"Duly noted," Todd said drily.

"We just have to stay cool if they ask *us* anything." And they dragged Squeers, wrapped in black plastic, out the door and down the corridor.

At the far back corner of the building they slipped through an unmarked door into a dimly lit space by a service entrance. They put Squeers down, caught their breath, and looked at each other. Each felt a *frisson* they could not explain. Todd felt aroused. Nellie wanted to kiss him. Both reactions were cut short by a voice, sweet but with an edge, speaking from a dim corner: "Good evening!" A figure stepped forward.

"Mrs. Bishop!" Nellie said.

Mrs. Bishop smiled. "I trust that you have some kind of permission to remove whatever-that-is from the building?"

The young people looked at one another. Nellie opened her mouth, could think of nothing to say, and closed it.

"What I mean," said Mrs. Bishop, "is that I *trust* you have permission. I *trust* you. So I am not going to ask to see anything. I am certain you are doing some kind of good work for the school. You always are. That's what I would tell anyone who asked. 'They do so much for the school.

41

They are our angels.' Well. I'm just going to go *lock up*." She stepped past them, toward the door from which they had just come. "If," she said, turning, "you know what I mean."

Todd and Nellie stared.

"And again," said Mrs. Bishop. "Anyone who asks, I will give you both the highest praise. I will say"—here she looked down at the package Todd and Nellie were hauling, and her voice turned bitter—"'They aren't like some people. Some people are mean and cruel. But not Todd and Nellie. Those two kids are the soul of virtue.'"

And she was gone, back into the dark school building.

CHAPTER SIX

An abrupt change of plan—A stroke of genius—
Like many a naïve youth before them,
our hero and heroine find themselves pulled into
a vortex of bloodshed and carnal desire—An affecting
account of that phenomenon known as "androphilia"

The headlights of Nellie's car illuminated an endless way between cornfields. The moon watched from behind a veil of silver. Dark barns blew by. A cozy farmhouse neared, a lamp and a TV on. Then it was gone. "So, we can count on Mrs. Bishop," Nellie said, and then she counted all the other ways their deed might be discovered and what the safeguard was against each one. "Except," she concluded, "you *have* been to reform school."

"But I found the Lord in reform school," Todd said. "Just ask Toby's parents. Trust me. Toby and his mom and pop know I am a virtuous boy now. What do you think I did in reform school?"

They slowed into a town tinier than theirs, its diner and tattoo parlor and soft-serve ice cream place closed. A banner over the main street promised an ox roast at a middle school.

"I dunno," Nellie shrugged. "I just figured reform schools can be—"

"I did what I always do," Todd said. "Studied. I took AP English and History. Plus Physics, French, and Pre-Calc. All A's."

"All A's," Nellie remarked ironically, "and yet you don't know enough not to murder someone in his own office!"

"Enough, already!" Todd said. "Oh, I also took Art. I made these awesome sculptures out of— Wait." He took out his phone. "I got an Instagram."

"*Plus tard*," said Nellie, though she found it sort of attractive that Todd had taken art classes and bothered to photograph his work.

They took a tight, blind curve, corn looming on either side, stalks suddenly bright and shadows twisted in the headlights, then pulled into another long straightaway. A sign loomed out of the dark: "Massauga Wetlands State Recreation Area." Fog stole through high grass. "There's a dirt road to the right," Nellie said.

"There!" Todd pointed.

Nellie turned. "We go about a mile in," she said. "Then we have to park and carry it—him—the rest of the way. It won't be easy. But no one will find him. Wait! What's this? The road's blocked." She braked and turned off the engine and the headlights. "Look. That's a backhoe, and a dump truck. There's *construction!*"

"There's a sign."

Nellie dug for a flashlight. "Go read." He opened the door. "And don't wave that thing around like we're signaling aliens!"

"Yes, ma'am." He stumbled forward to the sign, then cupped his hand over the flashlight and turned it on. A moment later he returned to the car. "Not good," he said, dropping into the passenger seat. "They're creating 20 miles of mountain bike trails, plus a campground and nature center. I'm guessing your drop-off site is not there anymore."

Nellie scrambled for her phone. She googled the state department of parks and read: "Fifteen-million-dollar investment . . . 20 miles . . . preserved for future generations . . . *Suck my dick!* What about *our* generation?" she huffed. "Okay, there's a map. The place I was thinking of is definitely gone." She minimized the map. "Almost eight. Where—? Dammit! I was counting on this! Plus there's this show I wanna see with Mom on PBS at nine."

"Know any other swamps?" Todd asked.

Nellie sat with her arms crossed and stewed. Finally, she started the car. "We can't sit around. The cops'll show up and put an end to the whole thing."

"Nells, I'm sorry."

"Don't dwell on it. Even if you'd done this the approved way, I'd have said dump the body here, and we'd be in the same pickle. Jeez, Mom must be wondering where I am. And I have a calc quiz on Friday. *Oh, my God!*"

"What? What now?"

"And a hundred friggin' empanadas to bake by Saturday. I totally forgot. How did this happen? Oh, wait. No. Yes. That's the answer. At least temporarily."

"The answer to what?"

"My bakehouse."

"Your who-what?"

"My *bakehouse.* There's not enough room in Mom's kitchen, so I bake my empanadas in that little apartment—over the garage? That's where we'll put him. You wanna watch TV with me and Mom? We'll stick him up there and then figure out what to do with him after."

"PBS might give us some pointers," Todd said.

"Don't laugh. I'm telling you, you watch enough *Father Brown* . . ."

45

Though the hour was late, Mrs. Lovett had changed into a bright red wraparound skirt and white blouse to greet Todd. "I realized," she said, wringing her hands, "I hadn't gotten out of my housecoat all day! Nellie, sweetheart, you must never let me do that again!"

Nellie hugged her mother and promised she wouldn't, ever.

It was not *Father Brown* that night but *Luther*, which Mrs. Lovett complained had "too much torture and dismemberment."

"Perfect for us!" Todd said. Nellie socked him on the arm. "Ow! I mean," Todd said, "it helps with, like, my Advanced Physiology course."

"Not that I can see that much of it," Mrs. Lovett added absently. Nellie took her mother's hand and kissed it.

When the show ended Nellie popped up. Todd stood, too. "We're just going out to the bakehouse for a minute!" she said.

"Nellie!" Mrs. Lovett said. "You're not going to stay up baking and then be too tired for class in the morning?"

"Mom, when has that *ever* happened?" She motioned Todd out the back door. "I do have to think about making empanadas for Saturday."

"You couldn't miss just one week?"

"Plus I might stay up to say hi to Dad. Toodles!" And she was out the door herself and closed it behind her.

They had deposited Squeers, still wrapped, in the center of the bakehouse floor. Nellie pulled a curtain with embroidered hearts and rainbows over the one small window. Then they just stood over the garbage-bag sarcophagus, illuminated by an overhead bulb in a frosted glass globe, dead moths and flies at the bottom. Worn, rickety cabinets ran around the perimeter of the room, most with doors that wouldn't close, and a stained sink, a Royal Rose stove, and a loudly humming refrigerator stood in one corner. A worn butcher-block table occupied the center of the room.

"If we could just somehow—" Nellie made vague motions with her hands. "*Compact* him or, I mean, he's big. There's a lot of him. Where are we gonna actually *put* him?"

"He's gonna start smelling pretty soon," Todd said helpfully. The refrigerator hummed.

"What we have here," Nellie said, chewing her thumbnail, "is a physics problem. He has to be converted into something."

"Well, you can't vaporize him!" Todd said. "I wonder, could you . . . maybe . . . if . . ." Todd sighed and dropped into a wobbly chair. "I'm such an idiot, I never should have . . . Nells? Nellie?"

She had stopped pacing. She stared at the Royal Rose stove.

"What?"

"We can't *burn* him," she said. She turned to Todd, a triumphant smile spread across her face. "But we can *bake* him! You're a genius!"

"Me? What did I do?"

"This week, for your gastronomic pleasure . . . Ashford Squeers empanadas!"

Todd's eyes popped. "Nells! That's impossible!"

"Oh, come on, everything's possible with a little imagination and a little elbow grease. I'll need your help. Are you in?"

"Wait. No! What about, like, the parts that"—Todd lowered his voice, though for whose sake he wasn't sure—"you can't eat?"

"Like what?"

"Like, not to be too explicit or anything, but, just as a for-instance, his liver!"

Nellie perked up. "And this week," she announced, "buy three empanadas and get a free slice of pâté!"

"Oh, my God! That is gross!"

"And brilliant! And P.S., if you don't like it, next time dispose of your own body!"

"I guess I do kinda have to step up here, don't I?" Todd admitted.

"It would help get it done by Saturday," Nellie replied. "You used to help me cut up apples. It's the same thing only a little more—"

"Human."

"I was going to say 'resistant.' But, yeah. No. Wait. Not human. Not him. What makes someone human? Compassion? Empathy? Curiosity? Take your pick. He didn't have one of them. He went around programmed to do one thing: evil. No, not human! Where's my cleaver?" She bustled from drawer to drawer. "I have a cleaver. Somewhere. And I'm sure there are YouTube videos on how to do this. I mean, to a cow or whatever. A 'human' can't be that different." She found the cleaver, then pulled her laptop from her backpack and set it up on the butcher-block table. She typed. "YouTube-dot-com. Here we go. 'Whole Cow Processed in Under 12 Minutes.'"

"Good!" said Todd. "I mean, the faster we get this done—"

Nellie shook her head. "Feels kind of overachieving to me. Like, 'Bro, I can do a cow in 12 minutes. I'm king of the world!' Dude's not into his *craft*. Okay, here's one: 'Home Butcher, 1,300-pound Cow, Warning: Graphic.' Ew!"

"Can we find one where the cow is, like, already dead?"

"Oh, no! Oh, Todd!"

"What?"

"'Methods to Slaughter Rabbits.' Scroll away, scroll away!"

Todd reached over and scrolled. "Here's one," he said, "'How to Butcher an Entire Cow: Every Cut of Meat Explained.' The cow definitely looks already dead."

"And it's from *Bon Appétit*. I love *Bon Appétit*. I feel like they'd, you know, be sympathetic. Click it."

"Okay, wait," Todd said, as the video began, "he's saying he's going to butcher '*half* a steer.'"

"And?"

"What about the other half?"

"Both halves would be the same, right?"

"I guess. Now, look, he's obviously already taken out the organs."

"That can't be too hard. In movies they kinda all come out in one sort of, like, *plop!*"

"Wait," Todd said. "This means we're going to have, like, by-products. Maybe we could market dog food as a side thing?"

"Park that idea," Nellie said, frowning at the video. "Now hold on. He's saying the shank is the most delicious. Remember that. We could charge extra for the ones made from the shank."

"I dunno," Todd said. "Squeers hasn't been grass fed. His shank might taste kind of gross."

"We'll use spices," Nellie said.

"What is a shank anyway? In, like, 'human' terms?"

"The calf. Sh-sh! He's explaining the eye-of-round."

A few more minutes and Todd asked, "Is this really so applicable?"

"It's giving me confidence," Nellie said. "The cuts may not be the same, but we're getting an idea what the process will look like."

"What about blood?" Todd asked. "Don't we have to, you know, drain him or something?"

Nellie covered her face and let out a resounding "Eww!" She paused the video. "Okay. Deep breath. I do have a couple of buckets. The vids about actual slaughtering would tell us, but I am *not* watching them. No blood, and no bunnies. Let's finish this and then we'll, I dunno, we'll figure it out." Their eyes met. Todd smiled. Nellie smiled back. Then she clicked and they continued watching. "Okay," Nellie said at the end. "Time to unwrap the product!"

The two of them stood over the garbage-bag-and-duct-tape bundle. Their eyes met again. Nellie's were bright and determined. Her mouth curled in a little smile. So did Todd's.

"I have a thought," said Nellie.

"I bet you do," said Todd.

"This is going to be bloody."

"Oh, John!" Todd mimicked Alice Morgan, the villain on *Luther*, "you're so brilliant!"

"Hardy-har-har! In order to avoid having to explain bloodstained clothes, I suggest we take everything *off* before we begin." Todd grinned. "Wipe that smirk off your face! This is business." Her mouth pulled into a sweetly smiling bud. "Mostly. Then afterward we use the outdoor shower, down there where no one can see, then we dress again, and voilà!"

"Sounds good to me," Todd said. He shucked his jacket and pulled off his shirt.

"Wow, Sweeney," Nellie said, pulling her own top off. "They must have had some gym at that reform school!"

"They did, actually." Todd casually caressed his pecs and abs. "A guy can't study calc all day, right?"

"Right. I bet you built up some, you know, 'frustration'?" She hesitated and looked down, then cleared her throat. "Could you, um, help me unhook this?"

"Sure." He stepped over Squeers's body, eased up behind her, and unhooked the bra. "And I did." His bare chest touched her bare back.

"Hair," she said, almost to herself, and smiled. She let the bra fall. "Did what?"

"Built up frustration."

She turned around, looked up admiringly and hesitantly, and then kissed him. Softly she said, "You're so nice," and kissed him again.

"A nice murderer," he said ruefully.

She looked up, eyes afire. "You did it to defend people." Her voice rose. "Vulnerable people we love. That's a lot more than nice!" They kissed some more, he cupped her breast delicately, and she asked, "So, any guy-on-guy action in there?"

"Well, I'd never, you know, with the young ones," he said. "They were segregated anyway, though I wouldn't trust those guards. But, hey, if a dude my own age was cool with it, and we were close. I mean, if it was someone I'd want to make feel good, why not?"

She nestled against him. They kissed and caressed lightly, holding back, letting the feeling build. "But I wanted something more."

"So what did you do? With these dudes your own age?"

Todd shrugged and grinned. "The usual. Stroking each other. Contests. Who can do it faster. Or shoot farther."

"Really?" Nellie tenderly caressed his biceps and then moved in for one long, deep kiss. When they broke she asked, "Did you win?"

Todd kissed back, long and hard. Then with a grin he said, "Usually."

"What else?" she sighed, nuzzling his collarbone.

"What do you mean, 'What else?' Like, sex?"

Caressing his nipple she hissed, "Of course like sex!"

"Sure," he sighed. Gently he kneaded her breast. He was fully hard.

"Seriously?" Another deep, wet, lingering kiss. "Actual sex?"

"You judging, Nells?" And another, longer this time.

"No! I guess I'm just, like, curious." An even longer, deeper kiss. "What did you do?"

Now he gave her tiny, tender kisses all over her face. "My roommate and I went down on each other," he said casually. "He was cool. It felt good to make a friend feel good."

"Were you naked?"

"Totally," Todd said. "Usually before a shower or after lights out. Or early, before dawn."

"What exactly did you do?"

Still kissing and caressing her, Todd went into detail about what he did with his roommate, what the guy liked best, what Todd liked in return, what they took the greatest care with, what they said to each other, and, of course, how it ended.

"You didn't!" Nellie said with a grin, blushing.

Todd crushed her to him, pressed his hips against her, and gave her a long, deep, insane kiss. "They had inspections," he whispered, panting. "You can't have 'em like, 'Sweeney, what's that on your sheets?' or 'What's all the tissues in the wastebasket?'" He undid his belt. Nellie knelt to help. "So you swallow the evidence. I mean, you're doing it for a friend as well as for yourself. It's bonding!" A pause as Nellie worked. Then, "Yeah, Nells," Todd groaned. "Yeah, just like that!" After a bit she stood and they kissed again, wildly. When finally they pulled back, she saw the question, gentle and tentative, in his eyes. She blushed and smiled.

"I guess," she said, batting her eyes, "it's about to get even bloodier in here!"

After a second Todd grinned. "Wait. You're kidding!" he said.

"Well, who has the time?" she demanded. "I'm president of this and fundraiser for that, and I take AP whatever, and it's like, okay, in all that I forgot to lose my virginity. Sue me!"

"I'm not going to sue you," Todd said softly. He leaned in. She went up on her toes. He whispered in her ear what he *was* going to do, adding, "If you want."

"Yeah," she said, breathlessly, nodding. "Oh, yeah, I want!"

"Wait just a sec," he whispered. He pulled a foil packet from his back pocket, held it up, and smiled. "Gotta make sure I got my goalie!" he said.

"Okay!" Nellie sighed, raising her naked body from the butcher-block table. "No more messing around. Jeez, look at the time! My dad'll be home. Get the cleaver over there, and that big knife."

52

A naked, still half-aroused Todd sauntered over to the knife collection.

"So," he said with a deep breath, "I guess, like, the head goes first, since you're not going to, you know, use it? And that way, we can, um, you know, drain the blood off so that—"

"Oh, gosh!" Nellie sighed. "Can we just—I'm sorry—use another word beside 'drain'? Like, maybe, 'separate out'? Or, wait, what's the French for 'drain'?"

"*Drainer*," Todd said.

"It would be."

Todd tapped his phone a few times. "In Esperanto it's *malplenigi*. How about that?"

"Oh, let's just—" She made a sawing gesture. "The head. You know." Todd reached for the cleaver. Nellie shook her head. "I can," she said. "There'll be plenty of wet work for us both. Get the pail."

Todd got the pail and crouched naked, holding it in position. "You look good like that," Nellie remarked. They grinned at each other, and then she surveyed Squeers's corpse. She breathed deeply and worried the handle of the cleaver.

Seconds passed. Then softly Todd said, "He wanted to rape my mother, ruin my best friend's life, ruin my life, and throw a refugee out of school."

Nellie gripped the cleaver.

"He said he was going to take my dad's place. Everywhere."

With a banshee cry Nellie raised the cleaver and brought it down on Squeers's throat. And brought it down again and again.

Moments later the head hit the floor with a thud. Todd raised the pail. As Squeers's blood was no longer pumping, it took some time. "Don't they usually hang the body upside down?" Todd asked. Panting, Nellie shook her head. "We don't have time. This has to be good enough." She peered around the pail and looked between Todd's legs. "Excites you, huh?"

"Actually, it's the blood on—" He cocked his head at her breast.

She looked down. "Dude, this is why we're doing it naked!" she said.

After what seemed like an eternity of bleeding, they set the pails aside. They spread the drained cadaver on the table and went to work, first with the cleaver, chopping off the limbs and separating the legs at the knees, then with the knife, slicing away muscles. The shoulders were most challenging. Both of them worked for several minutes around the scapulae. "Don't be so artful," Nellie said. "You're not selling Mrs. Bishop her Sunday dinner. This all goes in the grinder."

"There's still a lot of blood," Todd observed.

"Well, dab it up! Whatever! Speaking of the grinder, I'd better find it." Todd was momentarily distracted by how perfectly lithe and lovely she looked, crouching and stretching as she went through the cabinets, her bare back curved, her pale arms undulating as she dug through utensils.

The grinding was harder and took more time than they had imagined. They took turns, huffing and puffing. Todd thought it incredibly sexy how the sweat running down their bodies made bloody streaks. He wanted Nellie again when they were done. "Easy, cowboy," she said, caressing him. "The bad news is, to make it really good, you gotta put it through a second time."

"Oh, no!"

"It goes easier."

"Like, how could it not?" He kissed her. "You know what else you can put in a second time?"

"Definitely," she said, "but right now we have to hurry. My dad's gonna be home any minute. We can't bake tonight."

They decided Todd would do the second grind and bag up the "by-products," while Nellie cleaned the floor and then, as Todd finished grinding, went down to the shower behind the garage. She was fresh and clean in time to meet her father, rolling in late from his job.

"Hello, Kitten!" Mr. Lovett said, coming to his daughter with a slight limp. They hugged long and close. "You're up late!" he said, his voice gravelly and weary. He saw the light in the bakehouse. "Not sacrificing your studies to the pie business, are you?"

"I had some extra time after I finished my English essay." She reached up and held in her hands that face that had fallen so long ago, but that always managed a smile. "How are you, Daddy?"

"Oh, not too bad, tonight." The old man shook his head. "Seems there's a little bit less work each week, but . . ." He looked at her and frowned. "Why's your hair wet, Kitten? You didn't get all dolled up just for old Dad, didja?"

"What, this?" She felt her hair, as though surprised it was wet. "No. Just a long, hard day. Like you, Dad. I wanted a shower. Hey, I put your food in the microwave."

"Well, let's have at it, then! Say, Kitten, I thought I just saw a shadow up there in the bakehouse."

"A sha—? Oh, Todd's helping. We've got a lot to do this week!"

"Todd Sweeney?"

"Now, Dad!"

"That boy has been to reform school, Kitten! He's been in with hard-core—"

"Daddy!" She turned him toward the house, guiding him lovingly up the porch steps. "I've told you a million times, he was framed. He got all A's in his classes when he was in there. He's a good boy, Daddy. Have I ever made friends with a boy who wasn't good?"

"No you haven't, Kitten; you're very responsible." The old man removed his steel-toe boots, and he and his daughter went in. "Maybe I don't tell you often enough, Nellie. Your mother and I are awfully proud of you. You get A's, too, and

55

you raise money for those scholarships. And choir and athletics. We're very proud, and I don't mean to question your judgment. Especially since Todd's helping you raise money!"

"That's right," Nellie said brightly. She helped her dad off with his coat. "Now, let's get that dinner going!"

Todd was relieved that the meat went more easily through the grinder the second time. He had set the liver aside, as Nellie had requested. She was serious about making pâté. Now he looked at Squeers, ground up, lying in the pan, and thought how, a few hours before, this had been the most terrifying presence in his life and his mother's. And Toby's. And everyone's. Now that fearsome figure was hamburger. Plus some bones and intestines they had to get rid of. But with Nellie by his side, he could do it. She was so sweet and beautiful! He heard footsteps on the stairs. She swept in the door. She was flushed and her eyes sparkled. She had not put her bra back on; that and her wet hair made her look kind of wild and wanton.

"This is kind of cool," she said. "Me with clothes and you naked."

"At your service, ma'am," Todd said, touching himself lingeringly.

"I think I'll keep you like this for a while."

"Happy to oblige, ma'am."

She brought up the calculator on her phone. "Okay, this may be a bit daunting," she said, "but, if I base this on my usual recipe, we are going to need . . ." She looked at the pan of meat and made a face. "What are we looking at? Twenty-five pounds?"

"That's all?" Todd hefted the vat. Nellie watched his muscles work and looked at his bloody bare feet and his calf muscles bulging.

"Your head alone is eight percent of your weight," she

56

said. "Then minus the bones and stuff. I've gotta think about where to dump all that. I'll come up with something."

"Based on my experience weight-lifting in the slammer," Todd said, "I'd say twenty-five."

"Okay. So. We have to multiply by about twenty. Meaning we will need . . ." Todd watched her fingers dance over the calculator and remembered their touch on his back and shoulders. "Twenty-five onions, twelve-and-a-half cups of tomato sauce, twenty-five teaspoons of oregano and twenty-five of dill, twenty-five salt, plus a lot of pepper. And for the crust . . . wait for it. Six-and-a-half pounds of butter, more salt, and, fanfare please, a hundred and twenty-five cups of flour. Maybe Mom has coupons." She glanced at Squeers's liver. "The pâté, obviously, is a whole other thing."

Todd delicately hefted the organ. "Three pounds," he said, "give or take."

From a nearby shelf Nellie pulled *The Joy of Cooking*. "Pâté, pâté." She flipped to the recipe. "Much easier," she announced. "They say truffles, but that's too much upfront investment. Plus, too conspicuous. We'd be almost the only people buying 'em the whole week." She looked at the smears of blood on Todd's torso where he'd wiped his hands after hefting the liver. "Damn!" she whispered. Todd grinned. He leaned over and touched the liver again, then wiped his hands further down on himself. Nellie blushed and smirked. "Okay, we'll go to Kroger tomorrow and stock up, then bake tomorrow night," she declared. "Once we get going, it shouldn't be difficult."

Todd came up behind her and put his arms around her waist. "Like something else we did tonight," he said softly. "Once we got going—"

"Careful!"

"Oh, the blood. Sorry."

"Why don't I take you down for a shower?"

"That sounds nice."

57

"It's going to be more than nice."

"What if someone sees?"

"It's behind the garage. The only thing that might see is a raccoon!"

Between the dark forest and the rough wall of the garage, they stripped again, and she knelt for him, and he for her. As the water ran over them, Todd held Nellie's face in his hands and stared.

"What?" Nellie asked, smiling.

"My God!" Todd whispered, slowly shaking his head. "You just processed a whole human being in one night based on a YouTube video. You are so amazingly awesome!" He kissed her long and deep.

"You did it, too," she reminded him.

"It's *how* you did it," he said, breathless. "It was so . . . *smart*. It was so, like, *strong*."

She giggled, "Oh, you!" And she wrapped herself around him.

Afterward, they dressed, and Todd, having assured his mother twice via text that he really was on his way, got in with Nellie, and she drove him home. They kissed tenderly before he got out. "Now, sweetheart," she said softly. "Along about Wednesday, when they start wondering where Squeers is, don't say too much, but don't say too little." She smiled. "I already know what I'm going to say."

"What?"

"I'm going to announce an Ashford Squeers Scholarship. To be funded by the sale next Saturday of you know what!"

Todd grinned. "Brilliant," he said. "As always." He kissed her again, then got out, and as her car pulled away, he bounded up the front steps, breathless and elated that he had found a girl who understood him so perfectly.

At home, late, the town dark and silent under his window, Todd wrote:

Dear Trent –

Hey, man. I know it's been a while, but I was telling my girlfriend about you, tonight, kind of in detail, and it really made me want to connect with you again. Yeah, I have a girl now. She's beautiful and just really, really brilliant. More so than me—if you can imagine that! She's into charity work and takes care of her parents, who are going through really hard times. I love her, but when I talked about you and thought about you again, I realized this doesn't change what happened between us.

The main reason I'm writing is to tell you how much I love you, too. I love you so much, and I'm glad we were so close and that I have those memories. I love Nellie (that's her name), and I'm probably pretty straight or whatever, like you are, but it's so amazing to have a guy you can share that stuff with. I'll always think of myself as having a part of you in me, and I'll always think of myself as having left a part of me with you. I became a man with you, and you with me. We gave our manhood to each other and we helped each other grow. I'll never forget that. You're a generous, good man, Trent. Remember that, and remember me. I'll always remember you. Maybe we'll see each other again someday and renew our pledge to each other.

With love,
Todd

CHAPTER SEVEN

The scheme appears a great success—But the righteous,
charged with protecting our safety, have their suspicions—
A vicious threat is directed at young Tobias—
Our heroine promises a rendezvous in the deep,
dark wood, but it is not with our hero

"Empanadas! Fresh, hot empanadas!"

"What flavor do we have this week?" Principal Poindexter asked, holding out his two dollars. His shiny, pink face looked a bit drawn.

Todd panicked. They had never discussed this.

"Herbed chicken!" Nellie trilled cheerfully. She tossed her tresses adorably out of her face.

"Herbed chicken!" Todd echoed. "Yessiree!"

"Mmm! It's delicious!" Poindexter moaned. "Dear me. At least there's one piece of good news this week," he sighed, holding up the empanada. "Poor Mr. Squeers." He took another bite. "Such a rock of a man. A legend." He chewed. "And suddenly, missing. And blood"—he mouthed the word—"on the carpet! But no solid leads. Not a one!" Nellie took Todd's hand and squeezed it. "Mm-mm!" Poindexter said. "This is just *luscious*!" And off he sauntered, a satisfied customer. No sooner had he left, telling others along the way that they *had* to try this week's empanadas, than two more visitors approached. Todd recognized then: Officers John Doogan and Tarron Littey of the town police department.

"Mrs. Bishop said I should speak to you," Doogan said, "about the Ashford Squeers disappearance." Doogan was maybe twenty-five and still trying to look like a real police officer, arms akimbo, first one hip cocked, then the other, his hat aslant. "She claimed you were at the school the night we think it happened. Doing some kind of charity work?"

"Yes!" Nellie said.

While Todd's mind reeled at the thought that dear, sweet Mrs. Bishop might have betrayed them, Nellie pretended to think hard about whether or not they had seen or heard anything. She concluded that they had not.

"What about you?" Littey stared at Todd. Littey was older and less intelligent than Doogan. He made up for it by curling his lip—the repulsiveness of it enhanced by an untrimmed moustache with food in it. He emphasized his words by poking the air with his nightstick.

"I didn't hear anything," Todd said. "Or see."

Doogan brought up Todd's stint in boot camp. "Where I got all A's," Todd said, "and found the Lord." He put his hand over his heart. Nellie turned from the customer she was serving and nodded approvingly. "If I had even the slightest idea who might have done whatever to Mr. Squeers—" He remembered at the last minute what Nellie had advised, "Never describe the crime to the cops; you'll blurt out a detail they haven't released."

"—my conscience would not permit me to let that person escape God's justice."

Doogan nodded. "Still," he said, "you were no fan of Squeers. That's what we hear."

"No, sir, I wasn't," Todd said.

62

"So," Doogan said, "Did you *forgive* him?"

"It was very hard," Todd said. "I'd be lying if I said part of me isn't, well, almost relieved that he's gone. God forgive me."

"Well, there's an admission of guilt!" said Littey. He took a step closer to Todd. Clearly he had had scrambled eggs for breakfast. And a Scotch, if Todd's nose was not wrong.

"Anyone will tell you I didn't like him," Todd said. "And he didn't like me. I can't hide that. It doesn't mean I could ever bring myself to *do* anything to him."

"What I hear," said Doogan, "is that you blame him for putting you in reform school."

"No!" Todd said.

There was a silence. Nellie busily filled three orders almost at once.

"No?" Doogan said.

"No," Todd repeated.

"You don't."

"No."

"Not at all."

"No, sir."

"Well, we hear . . . but if you say no, I guess . . ." Doogan and Littey exchanged glances. Doogan turned back to Todd. "We'll be getting back to you," he said. Then he looked at Nellie and added, "Both of you."

"Would you like an empanada for the road?" Nellie asked. "Herbed chicken. It's for a good cause."

Littey read the sign aloud: "'Ashford Squeers Scholarship Fund.' Huh!" He looked at Doogan and shrugged. Doogan shrugged back. They each bought an empanada. They both bit in and—Todd suddenly realized—began consuming the evidence. Or at least some of it. Juice dribbled down their chins. "This is great!" Littey exclaimed, hurriedly wiping himself.

"Yeah," Doogan said. "What's your secret recipe?"

"Now, if I told you," Nellie said, batting her eyes, "it wouldn't be a secret, would it?" She turned to yet another customer. "Yes, ma'am?" she said. "I just bet you came for some nice herbed chicken, didn't you?"

When the cops finally left, Nellie and Todd both fell into the front seat of her car and slammed the doors.

"Oh, my God, that was close!" Nellie panted.

"If I told you," Todd cooed, "it wouldn't be a secret, would it?"

"Oh, please! They loved it!"

"They ate it up!" Todd said. They high-fived limply. From the window they checked every few seconds for customers. "Now what's the deal with Mrs. Bishop?"

Nellie narrowed her eyes and smiled. "She said that in case someone else said they saw us. Plus she made us look good with the 'charity work' thing. And of course she said she locked up Squeers's office herself and saw nothing. So it's actually brilliant."

"I hope so."

"And *you* were brilliant!" Nellie added.

"What? The part about 'God's justice'?"

"Yeah, but even better was admitting you hated Squeers. That's exactly how you do it. 'Fess right up. To *something else*. The best was when he asked if you blamed Squeers for reform school, and you're like, 'No.' And then, crickets!"

"Uh-oh," Todd said, looking out the window.

"What?"

"You got a customer. Ryan Plouf."

Nellie opened the door. "Ryan Plouf chewing on Ashford Squeers," she muttered. "How appropriate."

Todd brought down his window and watched. Nellie, poised defiantly, kept her answers upbeat and brief; Ryan, thumbs hooked in frayed belt loops, tugged at his crotch and fished two dollars out. He wolfed an empanada. Suddenly his face froze. His eyes went wide. He looked right at Nellie. His expression seemed almost human. He went for more money and stuffed in another empanada. He signaled to Taylor. Todd got out of the car. Just because Ryan liked the goods didn't mean Nellie was safe.

Now Taylor was also wolfing one down, and Nellie was selling both boys cider to boot. They bought four more empanadas to go. Then Ryan jerked his head at Taylor as if to say, "Scram." Taylor looked at Nellie, then Ryan, then loped off.

Ryan leaned across the table. He ran his tongue around his teeth and grinned at Nellie. His left eyebrow went up. Todd took a step closer but couldn't hear what Ryan was saying. Nellie stood frozen. Then, his index finger trained on Nellie like a gun, Ryan winked at her and backed away.

Todd strode up to her. Her face was white. "What did he say?" Todd demanded.

"You know what he said," Nellie answered quietly. "It's what that type always says."

"Did he threaten you?"

"Not in so many words. He wants a 'date.' He wants to show me he's a good guy and a 'real man.'" She put her arms around Todd, and he enveloped her in his. She nuzzled his chest. "You're the only one," she said. "The only one to be strong *and* good."

They did not have long to brood on Ryan's meanness. Word had spread how wonderful Nellie's empanadas were. Friends and teachers and out-of-towners they had never seen before bought one after another. "Great," Nellie said. "We raised plenty of money, but it's not like we can do it all over again next week. Guess it's back to leftover cheese."

Suddenly Ryan bounded toward them.

"Speaking of which," Todd said.

"Hey!" Ryan panted. "Did you talk to those cops? They

were just asking me about Squeers. How he disappeared and now there's blood in his office?"

"Oh, my God!" Nellie squeaked, and clung to Todd.

Ryan could barely speak for laughing. "So, I told 'em— Y'know that black kid? Ooga-wooga Unga-wunga or whoever?"

"Bamedele Cetshwayo," Todd said.

"I told the cops to look at him. I said I saw him sneakin' around. I mean, that's what them types do: sneak around. With, like, the really white eyes and how they don't talk to anyone. He probably won't get in any real trouble, but it'll send a message. Stay out of our town, boy! They'll let him go when they get sick of his accent. 'Hey, Ooga-wooga, whatcha think of *The Grapes of Wrath?*' 'Oh, doo-doo-doo-doo-doo-doo-doo-doo.' 'Hey! *Speak English, dude!*' I gotta go, but if the cops say anything to you, just say you saw Ooga-wooga sneakin' around. This is gonna be fun!" He was about to bound off when he stopped and turned to Todd. Abruptly he became still and focused. His eyes narrowed. "Speakin' of fun," he said. He scratched his stubble with untrimmed nails and belched. "You know your little *fag* friend?"

Todd felt as though electricity had shot through him.

"Next time Fleet wins a home game," Ryan said, "me and the guys're gonna take your friend down to the basement and celebrate. If you know what I mean. You can go ahead and tell him. He can't get outta it." He chortled, then frowned at Todd. "Oh," he cooed, "is Daddy gettin' upset? Is he scared for his little boy? What do you two do together, Sweeney? Ha-ha! Whatever it is, when we're done with that little princess, he won't be able to do it no more. 'Bye, Sweeney!" Then he leered at Nellie. "And you, think about my offer. Your *boyfriend* here doesn't look like he can really 'stand up,' can he? Catcha later!" And Ryan was off, again with a wink and his finger pointed like a gun.

Nellie clung to Todd and wailed, "Oh, my God! Poor Toby! And Bammy! We can't let this happen. We have to do something!"

"I think," Todd said, "that you need to say yes to that date."

"To *what*?"

"To that date with Ryan. You need to say yes."

Nellie's arms dropped and she stared. "Are you out of your mind? Actually go on a date with— What could you possibly mean? Plus, I thought we were together now. I mean—"

"You need to take him," Todd said slowly, "to some dark, secluded place . . ."

Nellie stared, incredulous, a tear running down her face.

". . . far from the center of town."

Still she stared, chin trembling.

"And there," Todd concluded, "you can have a conversation with him about the *meat* you're looking for. For next week."

Slowly an ever-so-slightly wicked smile transformed Nellie's face. She wiped her tears. "You might be right," she said.

"I'll come, too," Todd said, "so we can take a *stab* at the problem."

"I would call this more of a problem-*slash*-opportunity," Nellie said, snuggling up to him again.

He caressed her hair and kissed her temple. "I think," he whispered huskily, "that Ryan could be *filling*. An important role. For us."

Abruptly they kissed, hard. They were interrupted by customers who wanted to buy the last of the empanadas. "I'll pack everything up," Todd volunteered. "Why don't you go and tell Ryan that his dream is about to come true?"

Nellie rolled her eyes. "That's the problem with the Ryan type," she said. "They don't dream. Where should we go? Massauga Wetlands?"

"No one's gonna be there till the construction guys on Monday, right?"

"Right. But we're not leaving evidence this time, right?"

"Right. I guess."

"My hero!" She kissed him, took a deep breath, and ran off after Ryan.

Todd packed up the empty containers, folded up the card tables, and stowed it all in Nellie's car.

Nellie came back quickly. Stone-faced she said, "He didn't believe me." She dropped into the driver's seat. Todd got in beside her. "He said it had to be a trick."

"So what do we do?"

Nellie smirked. "Wait."

"For?"

"Can you imagine Ryan Plouf actually, in the end, saying no to sex?"

"Never."

"Exactly. Plus, I told him the offer was limited time only because you'd be away tonight."

"What? What else did you tell him?"

"Well, the words 'plow' and 'seed' were both used non-agriculturally." Todd's jaw dropped *"Kidding! Just kidding!* Everything I said was something I could repeat to the cops. I never actually said we were going to have sex. I never even said the word 'date.' 'Officer, I have no idea what Ryan could have been thinking! He probably wanted to impress his friends.'" Her cell phone lit up. "What did I tell you? Hello? Ryan!" A pause. "Honestly, I'm kind of hurt." Todd snorted. Nellie shushed him. "It made me think," she sighed, "that you don't like me. You just want to . . . *use* me!" A longer pause. Her face lit up and she pumped her arm. Then she slumped and sighed pitifully. "I just don't feel like it anymore," she whined. But when Ryan spoke again, she made a victory fist. When they finally hung up she spread her arms and cried to the heavens.

68

"What a tool!" she said. "He's gonna be there. *No matter what I say!* He's going to show me he's serious, if he has to stand out there alone all night."

"So, of course we'll be late."

"'But, Officer, you saw his texts: "Nellie, where are you?" "I'm all alone." Well, Officer, he was alone, because I wasn't there!'"

"You're dangerous."

"I know."

"I mean it."

"I know! Let's go have sex in the bakehouse."

"Right behind ya!"

"My favorite position!"

CHAPTER EIGHT

The threat to Tobias is removed, but at a great risk to the reputations of others—Androphilia is further elucidated

The young man's body lay twisted in the muddy track mark of a backhoe. Crickets chirped. A quarter moon shone down. He still had an erection, still clutched tightly in his fist. "It's that kind of thing," Todd lamented, pointing his bloody paddle at Ryan's hard-on, "that makes *us* look bad."

"Dude, precisely," said Nellie. "I try *so* hard to make things artful and discreet, and then this . . . "

"Oaf."

"Oh, my God, I love that word!" They high-fived. "This *oaf* makes us look like amateurs!"

"I think I might hit him again. Just for that."

"No! The blood spatter and everything." She sighed. "You know, I work hard!"

"The hardest!"

"I get A's, I look out for my parents, I raise money for charity—"

"You're, like, the Martha Stewart of Fleet High. With Eleanor Roosevelt and Lizzie Borden kinda thrown in."

"Oh, thank you, sweetie!" Nellie said, putting her arms around him. "You don't know how much that means, you saying that. And I don't mean to shortchange your contribution. You care about doing things right, too." She kissed him on the cheek. "You take the lion's share of the risk. If we were caught, which we won't be, you could be charged with murder."

"Yeah," Todd said, "but the butchering-people-and-grinding-them-up-and-baking-them-into-pies-sold-for-human-consumption thing wouldn't go over too well, either."

"Not when you put it that way! I mean, no mention of community service? Social justice? And P.S., zero—count it—zero academic credit. What if I want to be pre-med? I should have an edge."

"You'd be such a great doctor!" Todd said.

"You!" Nellie snapped. "You just want me to examine you!"

"No no," he said more softly. "I mean"—he took her in his arms—"I'd *trust* you." She looked up at him, face quivering, and gave him a long kiss on the mouth. "You should at least do a TED Talk," he added.

She giggled. Then her face went serious. "I'd call it 'The Power of Two,'" she said evenly.

"Aw, Nells . . ."

"Okay. C'mon. We have to do the nonglamour part now."

Todd got the garbage bags. "Just out of curiosity?" He pointed to Ryan's erection. "Does that go in the pies?"

"Y'know, I honestly don't remember," Nellie said. "Squeers's pelvic girdle is kind of a blur to me. With this dude, though, I'd say it would be fitting."

"So, some poor tool might've eaten Ashford Squeers's . . . poor tool?"

"More likely it was, you know, evenly distributed." She tore off a length of duct tape. "I like that our work is democratic. Tape the ankles together before we bag the legs."

They bagged Ryan, then carried him out to the road (they had taken care not to leave tire tracks), heaved him into the back of Nellie's car, put on their shoes (having taken similar precautions with these), got in, and headed for the bake-house.

"Fleet High," Nellie said wistfully as a dark silo rose against the dark sky. "I can't wait to get out of there."

"Some kids," said Todd, "go to schools named after pres-idents. We go to a school named after an enema."

"Says it all, doesn't it?"

"It's what I'm going to use as my defense."

"Like, going to a school named after an enema was traumatizing."

"Exactly. Are we gonna get naked again to cut him up?"

"Well, it *is* the best way—"

"Are we gonna, you know, *do it* before we start in on him?"

She smiled mischievously. "If you insist."

On the outskirts of town, they passed tiny motels with flickering signs. "Vacancy." "Vacancy."

"I was specially looking forward to it this time. I mean, my rival, dead in a trash bag clutching his dick while right in front of him I get the girl he wanted. Can we unwrap him first, so he can watch?"

"You men!" Nellie said, shaking her head. She took Todd's hand. "Yes, honey," she said, "we can unwrap him so he can watch."

Todd thrust vigorously. The table rocked and squeaked. "Hey, Ryan," he panted. "You watching?"

Ryan Plouf's corpse lay on the floor, erection still in hand.

"Oh, baby!" Nellie squeaked, "you're so much better than that big loser, Ryan."

"Hey, buddy," Todd said, "you shouldn't've told her you wanted to get 'baked.'"

"He said he was gonna show me a piece of meat like I'd

never seen," Nellie whimpered, "so mentally I started going through recipes!"

"Ha!" Todd bucked harder.

Afterward, Nellie traced circles and figure eights on Todd's skin with her nail and asked, "Whatcha thinkin'?"

After a silent moment, Todd looked down at Ryan and then away. "Dunno," he said. "It's just a little different this time."

"How so?" She cuddled close.

"Someone my age. A bad guy, I know, but his whole life in front of him. You don't know—"

"And what are the odds, Sweeney?" She spoke low in a quavering voice. "That guy planned to gang-rape your best friend. Shall I say it again? *Gang. Rape. Your. Best. Friend!* You know what rape does to people? Ten minutes with Ryan's buddies and Toby could end up swinging from a noose or bloody in a bathtub!"

"Nells!"

"*That* is what rape does to people. What I just said? Those are actual outcomes of people getting raped. If they survive, then maybe permanent physical injury. And there'd be zero sympathy from the parents. They'd probably blame *him* and hurry him to that conversion camp even faster. Now, Sweeney, you tell me what the odds are that, 'with his whole life in front of him,' Ryan Plouf would ever do any better than all that?"

"I know. But, hey, doesn't everyone deserve their 'shot at redemption'?"

"In movies, sure. In real life, no one can protect the Tobys and the Anthonys. Not teachers, not parents, not cops. You and I protect the widows and the queer kids and the refugees. And, may I remind you"—she thrust a finger at Ryan—"when we sell his meat, someone gets that extra little bit at college that buys books or gas or networking over a beer."

Todd nodded slowly. Then he smiled a little. "Hey, I got

a question for you," he said. "What did you ever do with Squeers's, you know, 'extras'? You know, entrails."

"Buried 'em," Nellie said. "Far, far away. I probably shouldn't tell you. Just in case. But I'm thinking, like, when vacation comes, we should look into some kind of dog or cat food thing, like you said. Hey."

"What?"

"Now I've got a question for you, big boy," she said. She combed her fingers through his chest hair, and he played gently with her breasts.

"Uh-oh," he said. "Is it gonna be more about my roommate in reform school?"

"Maybe."

He shrugged. "Okay. Hey, I got nothing to hide."

She looked him up and down. "Wouldn't want you to hide anything!" she said. "Anyway. Your roommate."

"Trent."

"You have a picture?"

"Sure!" Todd hopped off the table and pulled his phone from his pants. He tapped, scrolled, and held it out to her.

"Damn!" she said. She looked up. "You two made a handsome pair!"

"I guess," Todd laughed. "I will say Trent was a case of handsome is as handsome does. I forget what he was in for, but he really wanted to make it right. He worked hard and he prayed twice a day. Not like a big show; I didn't even notice at first. It was neat, though, when we slept together, how he'd pray with his hands folded on my chest. He was super decent to everyone. So, yeah, very handsome. But"—he took the phone back—"we haven't gotten to your question yet."

She watched Todd, naked, broad back arched, as he tucked the phone away. "So, did you guys do anything more than, you know, what you said last time?"

Todd grinned. "Remind me what I said last time?"

"Oral."

75

"We did that."

"So, did you, like, go to the next level?" She batted her eyes.

"You mean, real intercourse?"

She blushed. "Well, that's about the only next level there could be!" Todd nodded. Her eyes went wide. "Shut *up!*"

"Nells," he said, sitting by her and taking her hand. "I want you to think about a certain word. I want you to think about it *symbolically*, right?"

"Okay."

"'Seed.'"

"Ew! I hate it when guys say that. When some guy says, 'I wanna fill you with my *seed*'? Yee-uck!"

"So how many guys have actually said that to you?"

"None. I'm just saying."

"Anyway," he continued, with a little smile, "think of it like this: everybody has *seed* inside them. If you love someone—and I loved Trent and he loved me, and I love you, too, obviously—when you love someone, you want to share *that seed* with them. Friend, lover, husband, wife, whatever. And you want more than anything for them to give you *their seed*." She made a face. "What now?"

"Processing the word. Continue."

"Sometimes you can't literally do that. Or don't. But me and Trent, we could. Guys have a thing about their cum. Not just how it can make babies, but how it's a sign of manhood. Whatever manhood is to you. And it's natural to share that."

"But, wait a minute. What about rubbers?"

"Everyone's tested for HIV when they go in that place. Neither of us had it, and after— Does this bother you?"

Nellie shrugged.

"It actually wasn't the best part."

"God! Is there another level?"

"Lying there naked after and talking."

"Talking? About what?"

"Like, what two guys talk about. Sports, movies"—he grinned and reached for her breast—"even girls. And school and God and life and trying to be men. Good men. He even asked me to pray with him. I got into it. I prayed for my mom and dad and for Tobes."

"The screws didn't pull you apart?"

"We kept it down. Plus, we were known for good behavior, so they didn't watch us like they watched other guys. One night, Trent asked who I prayed for. I told him, and he said, 'You didn't pray for yourself?' And I'm like, 'Oh yeah. Forgot.' I was in there 'cause I was framed. I didn't think I needed to get straight. But he said, 'You're neglecting yourself. Being a bad guy didn't get you in here. But you still gotta be a better man when you get out.'"

"Wow." Nellie kissed his hand. "Does it feel good being out and doing something positive now?"

Todd nodded. "Yeah. You've shown me a whole new world."

"Good. I'm glad." She hopped down from the table. "Hey, we'd better get on with it. Rigor's gonna set in pretty soon."

"I'll get the knife and the cleaver."

"Help me get him up on the table first."

"Hey, how are we gonna stash the meat? If we turn him into empanadas now, they'll be stale by next week."

"I'm way ahead of ya, big boy!"

Todd took her in his arms and kissed her. "You always are. What's the plan?"

"Mrs. Twaddle, next door? She's a total food hoarder. There's lamb chops in her freezer from the Carter administration. I'm gonna ask her a wee little favor, just till Wednesday."

Next morning, Nellie stopped Mrs. Twaddle on her way to church. The latter happily agreed to let Nellie store "provisions" with her.

"You should label this," Todd said, as he helped heft the goods in. "If she mixes Ryan Plouf into her Hamburger Helper, it could go badly for us."

So Nellie wrote her name on lengths of masking tape and wrapped them around her bundles of Ryan. "Okay," she said, as she shut the freezer lid and restored the lock. "Now I've gotta get rid of the bones and stuff."

"You know," Todd said, "in addition to the dog food thing, we should make fertilizer."

"Wouldn't we have to buy mass quantities of ammonium nitrate? I don't want to attract any attention."

Wednesday night, Nellie retrieved Ryan from Mrs. Twaddle. Then they hit Costco for flour, butter, and tomato sauce. After midnight, they slid the final batch of empanadas into the bakehouse oven.

"Why is there a fleur-de-lis on one of them?" Todd asked.

"That's the one with his dick," Nellie said. She shut the oven door and sidled up to Todd. "You want it?"

Todd kissed her, long and lingering. "Let's split it," he growled.

"You mean," Nellie said softly, "pull it apart?"

"Yeah!"

"While it's still hot?"

"Yeah!"

"And what if it . . . drips?"

"Just . . . suck it up!"

The two then spent several passionate minutes together until the last batch of empanadas reached puffy, golden perfection.

CHAPTER NINE

A terrifying nocturnal ritual—Innocent lads tormented—
Heroines of stage and screen defiled—A perplexing array
of icons presented to tender and impressionable minds

Pounding fists. He had been dreaming of sweet Toby. Now
Anthony lay awake, his heart pounding along with fists on
the doors of neighboring cells. He kicked at his meagre
covers and struggled to breathe. Muffled voices, more
pounding. "In the hall! Now!" He rolled onto the cold floor.
What time was it? His joints ached from working all day
on his knees, scrubbing the kitchen floor, then hunched in
the yard, shoveling in rain that soaked him through. The
pounding came closer. Abruptly it landed on his door. The
lock was undone, the door yanked open. Cold, brilliant
light shot in. He was lifted and dragged so fast his bare feet
could not keep up.

In the corridor boys yawned and shivered. "*Attention!*"
Warden Bates bawled, his small, shaven head like a fist,
shouting. Black hair had begun to come in again, making
him look as though a shadow clung to him. The veins at his
temples pulsed.

Up and down the corridor, the assistants' shouts echoed.
"Everybody out!"

"Stand up like men!" Bates bellowed, strutting before the boys. "Whining, sniveling pansies! No wonder your parents wanted to get rid of ya! Stand up like men!" Anthony tried. He actually wanted to. But all his body wanted was to be back in bed, cozy and restful.

"Form a line!" the assistants snapped. What *time* was it? They had not been roused in the middle of the night before.

"Hup-two-three-four!" they screamed in the boys' ears. The line began to move.

They turned a corner down a wide hallway toward double doors that led to the playing fields. Outside, the roar of rain. But they were barefoot, dressed in thin pajamas. (Anthony had not been too sleepy to steal glances at the boys he thought had especially cute or manly feet.) With a crash the guards opened the doors. Cold rushed in. "Go go go go go!" they bellowed, shoving boys or striking them with batons.

At first the boys hesitated, unable to believe they should go out in the pouring rain. But the shouting went on: "Go go go go go!" And so they ran, stumbling into the deluge, slipping, cutting their feet, twisting their ankles. Some cried out. Anthony made out a low cinderblock building up ahead. He pumped his legs, but it drew no closer. If only they would stop shouting. If only his mates would stop embarrassing him with their whimpers. Would it be so hard just to *go*, like the voices said? Then maybe they would stop.

The building loomed, windowless. Anthony did not like the look of it. It felt dead. Two small, weak yellow lights lit the outside wall.

"Halt! *Line up!*" The rain poured down. They formed a line. Some looked like they didn't care what happened to them.

Some boys were crying. Did they have to do that? Anthony wanted to shut their mouths himself. Didn't they know this would make it worse for everyone?

"Chins up, fellas!" a guard sneered. "Mr. Bates has an announcement for you!"

Bates strode through the rain as though it didn't even touch him. Not just his purplish-red lips were twisted in contempt, but his entire face. "That's right, fellas," he announced, coming to a stop and standing tall with arms folded, not making eye contact with anyone, "this is a special night. Tonight, you will begin the next phase of your recovery. You will be introduced to our reprogramming center." Anthony looked at the low, windowless building. What was in there? "The Bible tells us," Bates thundered, as rain poured down, "in First Corinthians, Chapter 13, verse 11: 'When I was a child, I spoke as a child. But when I became a man, I gave up childish ways.' Tonight, you will begin giving up childish ways." As they listened they shivered, their teeth chattered, and they wiped cataracts of water from their eyes. "By dawn, you will be repulsed by your childish ways. And you will start to become men." He waited. Anthony tried through the curtain of stinging rain to study Bates's uniform. It was dry! In all this torrent, it was perfectly dry. This man was the devil! Should he run? They'd catch him in a second. But he was about to enter the devil's lair.

"Open the doors!" Bates howled, and so the building's doors rolled back, screeching and grinding. Shoved and shouted at, the boys were herded inside. They slammed into one another and stepped on each other's feet. Elbows dug into ribs. Heads hit the wall. Someone called someone a "faggot."

Anthony heard another door open with a clang and a thud. "One at a time!" the guards barked. Anthony inched forward. He was dizzy. What awful machinery was inside? What spikes or straps or chains? What fate awaited them? Closer he came. The interior emitted a red glow, warm but menacing. Pushing and stumbling. "Get off me, faggot." And then, there it was!

81

A movie theater!

Just a movie theater! Already some boys were being pushed into seats. Anthony scoffed and shook his head. All that worrying about a movie theater. "Reprogramming," ha! They were just going to show some movie about how to walk and talk like a man. Just as boring as school back home!

Anthony was hurried to a seat, and now he noticed that the guards were fixing some kind of mechanism to the boys' heads. Boys were squirming and saying, "Ow!" The guards were wrestling them and attaching some kind of electrodes. A hand fell on Anthony's shoulder. He dropped into a seat. His wet pajamas squished. Hands went to work, and now, to his horror, he discovered what the other boys were complaining about. Some kind of headset was being strapped to his head. He tried to reach for it and say "Stop!" but they swatted his hands away and strapped his wrists to the arms of his seat. On each side of the headset were clips. Filthy fat fingers pulled Anthony's eyelids back. He tried to twist his head away as the clips came closer and touched the surfaces of his eyes. "No!" he gurgled. "No! Help!"

The clips locked into place, holding his eyes open. He could not blink. He felt as though he could not breathe. Like his comrades, he could only moan and gasp. One of the guards dripped eye drops in their eyes. The lights dimmed. Music played.

For a moment Anthony forgot his torments. The straps and eye clips and the moans of his comrades became bearable as he was lifted up above the earth.

For the melody was his favorite in all the world. "The Sound of Music." The camera floated over the mountains. Green fields, white flowers, babbling brooks. As the music built, here came Julie Andrews, carefree and ecstatic, striding through the grass, twirling, about to sing, and—

Wait. What was happening?

The music was now unnaturally loud. And as Julie Andrews began to sing the picture changed. What was that? A riot? And in the middle of it, an animal's face. A pig, terrified. Over Julie Andrews's voice, the screaming as the knife cut into the pig's throat. All the boys cried out. One screamed, "You can't!" and writhed in his restraints. The pig's blood spouted out. The men stabbed and hacked. And Julie Andrews sang about her heart being lonely. Anthony could imagine no heart lonelier than his. Except poor Toby's! What if Toby knew this was happening? It would break his heart. And that broke Anthony's heart doubly. He could have gone through this alone, but to think of Toby ever seeing or even thinking of this—

Julie Andrews's voice faded. The pig slaughter ended with an inverted, draining carcass and guys bloody and grinning.

Next there came the beautiful, low chords Anthony had heard a hundred times. It couldn't be! They couldn't do that. But they did. The voice of dear, sweet Idina Menzel, to whom he had practically prayed at night because he knew she would understand—that crystalline voice sang how something had changed within her. The music gathered momentum. Idina sang how it was too late to go to sleep. Then as her voice defied gravity, there came on the screen pictures of soldiers being machine gunned. Kristin Chenoweth joined in, and the bodies piled up, and boys wept openly. How could they do this? Couldn't they just have this one thing, this thing that had been given to them, this thing they had counted on, this thing without which life would be meaningless? Hadn't a real man written that song? Weren't there real men in the show? Didn't real men see it? Maybe it was just dads bringing little *girls*. Maybe that's all he was. A *girl*, pinned down and forced now to see life as it really was. Anthony wished Idina would come to him now. Or Kristin Chenoweth or Jeremy Jordan or Billy Porter or Barbara Cook or any of them. When he felt awful

83

and tiny and afraid, they had been there for him. They told him there was magic to do. They told him to seize the day and fight for a place in the sun and live forever. He streamed it all, because his parents would throw out CDs, and they set his computer up not to download from any site with anything good.

Now the music itself had been destroyed, a leering skeleton exposed. What a fool he had been to think you never walked alone. Or that there was a world he longed to see. Or to think that life would be a celebration, with Toby on his arm. Oh, God! What if they ever sent Toby to a place like this? He felt as though he'd been punched in the gut. He'd die before he'd see Toby in a place like this!

Finally, there came relief. Or what seemed like it.

The lights came up. The eye clips were removed. But the boys remained strapped in their seats. Bates paced back and forth and addressed the group.

"I trust," he sneered, eyes gleaming in cold amusement, "that our little show made you see the light. Those mincing 'show tunes' you love are so much vanity. The people who wrote them? Some are like you. The way you are now. But not the way you will be. You will be real men. The losers who go around sniveling about"—his voice went high and whiny—"defying gravity, some enchanted evening—they're going to hell! That is why we poison them in your minds, cleansing you, freeing you to contemplate how you can fulfill true virtue and manliness.

"And to help you a little further," he continued, and now the guards made their way through the rows, reattaching eye clips to the sound of groans and protests, "we have another film for you." Groans all around and cries of "Ouch!" and "Oh, God! My eye!"

"No. No." Bates stopped and held up his hand. "This film will be easier on the eyes. We showed you that other film because we care about you. We care that your mind is not

84

infected with the germ of homosexuality." Anthony had to wonder about the logic here. Why were conservatives always so hard to follow? "We care that you understand who your 'heroes' really are," Bates went on. "Leonard Bernstein! Homosexual! Cole Porter! Homosexual! Crushed by a horse, by the grace of God!

"Now we are going to show you some positive role models. Real American men. Working. Sweating. Building. Fighting. Winning. Doing what men do."

A guard clipped Anthony's eyes open. He resisted less this time. It was almost over. The lights went out. If he just got through this, he could sleep. Eye clips weren't the worst thing that could happen to you. Again, he wished the more vocal boys would shut up. Out loud he said, "Can't we just get on with it?"

The theater filled with the booming, blasting sound of a marching band. The screen flashed a bright blue sky. Fighter jets tore across it and a chorus of men sang,

> *Off we go, into the wild blue yonder, climbing high*
> *into the sun.*
> *Here they come, zooming to meet our thunder, at*
> *'em boys, give 'er the gun!*

There followed a cavalcade of airplanes, pilots, tanks, soldiers, cowboys, race cars and their drivers, football players, ironworkers, sailors, explorers, and who knew what else. Anthony recognized Charles Lindbergh, Theodore Roosevelt (twice), Matthew Perry, and both President Bushes.

But there were some strange images, as though the maker of the film hadn't checked with Bates. Naked guys horsing around in a locker room. Anthony had seen whole gay Tumblrs devoted just to that. A guy posing in a shiny jockstrap. He knew that style came from gay magazines back in the 1950s, when you had to make it look artistic.

85

Then there was Greg Louganis, who was gay. Heath Ledger and Jake Gyllenhaal in *Brokeback Mountain*. They looked manly, but didn't Bates know what that film was about? There was a whole sequence of upright-looking religious people, but the two Mormon guys were eyeing each other . . . Holy crap! They were from mormonboyz.com! He'd jerked off to it! He especially liked Elder Gardner and Elder Lund. He couldn't remember which was which, but who cared? The film returned to Mel Gibson and Mark Wahlberg and Dick Cheney and Alex Jones. The eye clips began to hurt. The music was weird, too. After the Air Force song came the overture to *Gypsy*—also stirring, but wouldn't it belong, in these people's minds, with the first film? Here it was played under pictures from . . . Abu Ghraib? Anthony also noticed that, in one picture of brave, manly exploration, some of the brave men were dead, their ships smashed by ice. He knew from history class that some of the manly fighting men they showed were Nazis and Confederate generals. The only black guy in the whole thing was O. J. Simpson. It was his mug shot! Then shirtless guys exercising. Anthony knew from the looks they gave each other that the pictures were lifted from porn sites. Now, "This Land Is Your Land" played. Anthony wanted only to close his eyes.

In the last shot, an American flag waved in the breeze, accompanied by a marching band playing "YMCA." Anthony was too tired to question it. Couldn't they just take the clips off?

At last they did. Moans rose from the exhausted boys. They hauled themselves to their feet as the guards barked at them to shut up.

Outside, the rain fell more softly. Anthony rubbed his eyes, but the hurt didn't go away, as though something were still stuck in them, like sand or burrs.

The dormitory corridor was actually a welcome sight. A clock said 3:00 a.m. Was that all? But they had spent a

86

lifetime in that theater. The guards herded them to their rooms. The lights were bright. Wouldn't they ever go out? Darkness. He just wanted darkness.

Instead, there came the final assault. With the dormitory lights glaring, stabbing their eyes and illuminating every corner, the PA system suddenly blared the overture to Wagner's *Flying Dutchman*. Bates walked up and down and shouted to the boys that, "throughout history, the greatest and manliest men have loved the music of Richard Wagner."

Anthony lay on his bed and covered his eyes. He could deal with this. He could bear up. He should just be glad that that other torture was over. He would do whatever he had to, never to endure it again.

CHAPTER TEN

Is no spectacle more affecting than that of a mother mourning one of her own?—Yet does that maternal mind not also harbor irrational fears and a repellent and willful ignorance?—A guardian of the peace intrudes—Tobias is distraught over those who would seek to alter his very soul

Nellie and Todd parked on the grass at the farmers' market, took Tupperwares and folding tables from the car, and set up the stand. Today was Fleet High Homecoming, so Nellie placed little mini-tiaras on the top layer of empanadas. She tied on a clean apron over her clothes. The townspeople, savoring memories of Ashford Squeers, descended on the mound of warm, plump pockets of Ryan Plouf's flesh. The air was filled with sighs and lip-smacks and slurps as people sucked up the juices, and belches as they finished, satisfied. Todd and Nellie graciously received the crowd's praise, briskly collected bills, and listened carefully for gossip about Ryan's disappearance: "I bet it was the African kid!" "But they let him go. He had nothing to do with Squeers." "Don't mean he ain't involved in this!" "Bet someone from the U kidnapped him. They take kids down there and make 'em gay!"

The pile of empanadas shrank. Nellie suddenly looked up. "Uh-oh," she said. "We should have thought of this."

Across the way, Ryan's mother and her other two sons, Dom and Woof (Woof's real name was Pulsifer), were getting out of their pickup. Dom attended to his mother, who was ashen and stoop-shouldered. She was also, Nellie noticed, going bald. Her nose was red and misshapen, and she wore a sweatshirt with red, white, and blue elephants and the words "I raise my children RIGHT!" Dom pointed her toward the empanada stand. Woof hovered behind, scowling and scratching his belly. He had a red blister under his eye.

"But," Nellie said, "I guess we have a reputation now."

Todd felt a jolt. Here she was, coming right at him, in the flesh, as it were: the grieving mother. And he was responsible. He had taken her son. Dom, in his "White Lives Matter" T-shirt, pulled his mother up to the booth. Woof straggled behind in a too-big T-shirt that said "My Indian Name Is Runs with Beer." Those nearby drifted off, not wanting to speak to or listen to Mrs. Plouf. She had been vocal all week about the "immigrants" responsible for her son's disappearance. "Hello," she sighed to Todd and to Nellie. She forced a half-smile. Her eyes were rimmed with red. "I hear these are real delicious," she said.

"You want one, Momma?" Dom asked. Woof was occupied with his phone.

"I don't know if I can eat," Mrs. Plouf said. "I can't eat, I can't drink, I can't sleep." To Nellie she said, "You know, A-rabs took my Ryan!"

"Did they?" Nellie said.

"They drink Christian blood," Mrs. Plouf said. "Reverend Hovadina said so. And my Ryan, he was such a good Christian, they just had to have his blood." Her face folded and she went weak in the knees. "What am I going to do?" she wailed. Woof watched his brother hold his mother up.

"I say it was the African kid," Dom sneered when his mother had righted herself. "Prob'ly some kinda voodoo. They oughta drag him in front of the whole town for a beating!" He caught Nellie's eye. "Yeah, you types are all wound up about 'social justice' and 'due process.' Good old-fashioned beatings do it every time." He turned to his mother. "Plus I told ya, Ryan shoulda been carrying a gun!"

"I know, I know," Mrs. Plouf whimpered, as though each breath were a chore. "Could we just get—" She turned to her boys. "You all want one of these?" Dom said, "Yeah, sure." Woof rolled his eyes. "Three of these pies," Mrs. Plouf said. "I know you all call them some fancy 'Hispanic' name, but anyone with half a brain knows Americans invented pie."

"We sure did," Nellie said, as she passed Mrs. Plouf a warm, golden packet of her son's flesh, and a napkin. "And one for Woofy," she added, "and Dom, this is for you." Todd saw Nellie hand the empanada with the fleur-de-lis to Dom. He watched, riveted, as Dom took a bite. A squirt of grease shot out and hit his mother's sweatshirt. "Sorry, Momma!" he said. "It's all right," his mother sighed. "I can Shout it out." She dabbed at the grease and began to cry. "But no detergent can bring my baby back!" She took another bite of her empanada and pulled herself together. "Now, I do have a question," she said, as she fished a five and a one from her fanny pack. "Can I say which of your scholarships my money goes to?"

Nellie stopped. A.) No one had asked her this before; and B.) Mrs. Plouf was chewing with her mouth open, and it was strangely riveting to Nellie to see Ryan Plouf going back, more or less, where he came from.

"Because I don't want my hard-earned dollars helping some illegal immigrant who kidnapped and tortured my poor Ryan!"

"You know," Nellie said slowly, "I think under the circumstances you all should not have to pay. At a time like this—"

"Oh, I insist," Mrs. Plouf said. She dabbed some more at the grease stain. "I'm not prejudiced. I just think white people should get a fair shake every now and then."

"After all," Nellie said brightly, "we invented pie."

"That's right!" Mrs. Plouf said and almost smiled. Nellie looked at Dom. His empanada had fallen apart in his hand, and he was awkwardly licking and slurping at his brother, some of whom fell to the ground. Woof played with his phone and nibbled at his empanada. "What about that boy Craft Speedwell?" Mrs. Plouf's eyes lit up and fairly danced. "I'd love to give him a scholarship!"

"I think," Nellie said, "that his family is pretty well off."

"I'd just feel all warm and runny inside," Mrs. Plouf went on, "if Craft Speedwell used my money to get ahead."

"Craft Speedwell's a dick," said Woof.

Dom smacked his brother and said, "Shaddap, douche-tard!"

"I *love* watching him play basketball," Mrs. Plouf said. "The way he shoots up in the air. Just shoots right up! And stuffs that ball real hard into—"

"He's a faggot!" said Woof. Dom smacked his brother again and his empanada fell to the ground. Nellie couldn't help but think, *Show some respect! That's your brother!* Mrs. Plouf interrupted her reverie to shout at her boys and to buy another empanada for "poor Woofy." To Nellie she confided, "Ever since his brother disappeared, the poor thing has had these big pustules on his you-know-where."

"Shut up, Momma!" said Woof. Dom smacked him yet again.

"Plus, he sweats," said his mother. "Goes through three, four shirts a day."

Woof wound up and hurled his second empanada halfway across the field. Dom seized him. Mrs. Plouf yelled at both boys.

92

"Ma'am?" Nellie asked helpfully, "how about a free slice of pâté to go with those em— I mean, those pies you have there."

"Pâté?" Mrs. Plouf demanded. "Ain't that French? You know, those people don't—"

"Not this pâté!" Nellie smiled and fairly sang the words as she held the pâté up for Mrs. Plouf's inspection. "This is Christian, American pâté. Guaranteed. Here."

Mrs. Plouf took a slice in her short, pointy fingers. "Well, it is good!" she said sweetly. "Mm. I could go for a slice, sure! You know, that Craft Speedwell is Homecoming King!" She closed her eyes, smacked her lips, and sighed, "Oh, that is heavenly!"

Woof peered at the pâté and said, "Hope the guy who ate it first liked it!" Dom curled his lip at him.

Mrs. Plouf's eyes popped open. "And the Queen," she whined, "is some *immigrant* girl. They probably had to do it. To get *funding* or something."

"Instead of inheriting it like the Speedwells did," Nellie said cheerfully.

Eyes closed, Mrs. Plouf put each finger in turn into her mouth, all the way up to the knuckle, and slowly withdrew it. "Just heavenly!" she sighed.

At last the three Ploufs made their way off, munching, Dom smacking Woof every few seconds.

Soon the empanadas were gone. Nellie and Todd sat in the car counting money. "Okay," Nellie said, "right here are the actual, physical eight dollars Mrs. Plouf gave me. What are we doing with it?"

"Road trip," Todd said. "To the state capital."

"Why?"

"On Fariss Avenue, by the statehouse, there's a synagogue. Synagogues have these things called tzedakah boxes, where you put donations. The boxes have different sections for different causes. So if you have, like, Jewish people helping African refugees, we get to offend Mrs. Plouf twice."

They agreed this was a perfect solution. For a moment they sat silently. "You know," Nellie said, "people are strange."

"No shit," said Todd.

"Your last name is 'Plouf,' okay? So you go and name your kid 'Pulsifer.' 'Pulsifer Plouf.' Say it a few times. No, don't. Then you call him 'Woof.' It's like a roadie name."

"It's child abuse."

"Totally."

"Would it be too much for us to whack the mother and the big brother, too?"

"I can't," Nellie said. "I have a history test Wednesday. Plus, it would start to look suspicious."

Suddenly there was a knock on the driver's-side window.

"Oh, hi!" Nellie said, rolling it down. Officer Littey put his thin-lipped face down and attempted a smile. He said, "Someone saw your car out by the Massauga Recreation Area the night Ryan Plouf disappeared."

"Oh, sure," Nellie said. "We were there."

Littey blinked. "Uh, you were?"

"Yup, that exact night." She leaned toward him, eyes wide. "Freaked me out when I heard!"

Littey's mouth opened and closed; nothing came out.

"We were sort of looking for, you know, a 'Lover's Lane.'" She glanced at Todd bashfully, then *sotto voce* asked Littey, "Do you have a girlfriend, Officer?"

"Huh?" Littey backed away. "Um, not at the moment. Listen—"

"Just don't tell anyone," Todd said. "Our folks are religious."

"Anyway," Nellie interrupted, "we were almost there, and we pulled up a map on the phone, right? That's when we found out about the construction. So, we just turned around. I have no idea where Ryan was."

Bemused, Littey attempted a few more rather unfocused questions, which Todd and Nellie answered without hesitation but with a great deal of beside-the-point chat. Finally Littey ran out of ideas. He drew himself up and informed Nellie that she had to move her car because there was no parking—right there where a dozen other vendors had parked. "Great minds think alike!" Nellie chirped, and started the car. Littey tipped his hat and turned to go.

No sooner had Littey disappeared than something hit the passenger window with a thud: Toby, tears streaming down, mouth stretched in agony as he sobbed, "Help! Please! They're gonna do it!"

"Get in the back!" Nellie called. Toby dove in. Todd reached and took his hand. "Whatsa matter, Champ?" he said.

"I'll never survive!" Toby wailed. "I can't stand it! I wanna die!" He went on to explain that his parents had at last arranged to send him to gay deprogramming camp. Not where Anthony was, but a place called Gethsemane, in the next state.

Nellie reached her hand back and laid it on Toby's head. "Sweetie," she said, "thing number one: shush. If we're going to fight this, we can't have people overhear you talking to us, okay? Like, especially the cop who just left."

"Okay," Toby whimpered.

"Number two," Nellie said, "no one is going to take you to gay conversion camp."

"Promise," Todd added.

"Promise," Nellie echoed.

"But how can you promise?" Toby wailed.

"Sh-sh-sh-sh-sh!" said Nellie.

"You can't beat these people," Toby moaned. "They always win. They're mean and they don't care what they do. They hate us and they want to just punish, punish, punish us forever!"

"Can we please stop," Nellie suggested, "fantasizing about 'forever' as though it has all already happened? Fact: I have a history test Wednesday. Fact: the two of you have stuff to do, too. May I suggest we stop wailing and worrying about the future, get our books, spread them out on my bed upstairs at home and do some actual studying, so that, years from now, when these petty problems have subsided, we do not end up being ignorant twats who actually believe Americans invented pie and African refugees are stealing whatever?"

Then to Todd she added, "This will also give us time to figure out what to do. But one thing I know: Toby, you are not going to any conversion camp." Toby still shivered and sniffled.

Todd got out of the passenger seat, got in back with his friend, and held him. "I'm gonna protect you, buddy," he said. "So long as I am in this world, you got nothing to fear."

Nellie wiped a tear away and said, "Me, too. Now, let's get in gear."

On the way to the Lovetts' house, Toby told them how a representative of the conversion camp would pick him up at his house Tuesday after school. The three of them spent a tense, at times tearful afternoon in Nellie's room, attempting to study.

By promising "a prayer vigil for his immortal soul," Todd convinced the Raggs to let Toby stay at his house that night. By dropping dark hints about what Toby was going through at home, Todd convinced his mother to look after the boy while he snuck out with Nellie, "to plan this big event for school."

CHAPTER ELEVEN

*Our hero and heroine plot a deception of a most
sexual nature—In the course of which we see how
needful are some for even the slightest ray of hope to
enter their tormented and constricted lives*

They sat in a booth at the Sweet Deal Diner. The walls were
hung with paintings of barns and waterfalls and with old
farm tools—rusty axes, saws, hatchets, and rakes. The
coffee came in thick, white ceramic mugs. Three old men
murmured and coughed and chortled at a table in the
corner. They remarked to the young server how "hot" her
coffee was and kept asking for more, even though they
hadn't drunk what they had. An older woman in an apron
said, "Don't worry, hon. They're just talkin'."

"So what we know," Todd said in a low voice, "is that
someone's coming to the Raggs' at 2:30 next Tuesday. We
don't know who. We don't know anything about them."

"Actually, we do," Nellie said, dribbling a little container
of half-and-half into her coffee. "Whoever it is makes their
living alone on the road for days at a time, picking up
young gay men and driving miles with them alone to this
conversion camp. Who takes a job like that?"

"A closet case," said Todd.

"I love you," Nellie said. They interlaced fingers and kissed. "So, this is not a happy, healthy man who marches in parades and wears a rainbow necklace?"

"Negatory."

"Perhaps this is a dude married to a woman with two-point-four kids and a house and recycling bins and a tree guy coming next week?"

"Positutely."

Nellie took a sip. "Then, gosh darn it, how does this upstanding married daddy ever enjoy a dinner of tubesteak and eggs?"

"When the tree guy comes, he stays home from work sick."

"Good. But will the tree guy satisfy him?"

"Nope. He'll be fifty pounds overweight and when he bends over to, y'know, do tree-related stuff, he has this big, hairy ass-crack."

"Right."

"Which will have dingleberries."

"Ew!"

"And lint."

"All right, all right! And so what does our guy do instead?"

"He hits the road. Plus, the nose hairs are probably—"

"I got it! He hits the road, desperately hoping—?"

"For a sign from God. That says, 'Rest Area, One Mile.'"

"And, Love-drops, what does he find at that rest stop?"

Todd slumped in his seat, squeezed his crotch, and growled, "Dude, wanna get some Oreos from the vending machine and have a party?"

They high-fived. The young server stole a look at Todd and he quickly sat up.

"So, seriously," Todd said. "You're using *me* as bait in a highway rest area?"

"Score one for you," Nellie said.

"But wait. Thing one: Like we said, we don't know who this guy is or where he'll be when. What if—?"

Nellie tapped her phone. "That's why you're gonna place a personal. *After* we call and confirm when he's coming."

"Gonna do your impression of Toby's mom?"

"Yup. And whoever answers is going to believe me. Because I'm going to tell them how much I want my little boy reformed. Same way this dude will meet you at the rest stop—because you're going to tell him what he wants to hear."

They paid the check. As they turned to go, one of the men in the corner asked the server, "You wanna hot me up? Huh? Wanna hot me up?" Nellie turned.

Todd gripped her shoulder and said quietly into her ear, "He'll say, 'You don't mind, do ya, sweetheart?' and she'll say, 'Uh-uh,' and after we go he'll start doing it double."

Nellie slumped. "Fine," she said. Outside she yanked open the car door and muttered, "Too old and tough for pie, anyway."

Huddled in the front seat of the car, they dialed the conversion camp.

The number went to voicemail, which gave an emergency number. "Like, if your kid just suddenly starts doing ballet?" Todd said. Nellie smiled sadly and dialed again.

"Hello? Gethsemane? This is Mildred Ragg, little Tobias's mother?" she said. "As you know, we are in *desperate* need. I have prayed and prayed for Tobias to see God's light. I know your program will help us. Now, as to the time you will be picking him up?" A pause. "And the gentleman's name? Mr. Sturbridge. All right. Will he be alone?" Another pause. "Thank you. And finally—I know this sounds peculiar, but I am sure you will understand— we have had a number of robberies and assaults in our neighborhood." In a stage whisper she said, "You know, *refugees. Mexicans.* Build the wall, I say! So I refuse to open the door now to anyone I do not know. So if you could tell me the type of car this Mr. Sturbridge will be driving, so I can be certain that it is he?"

99

"'That *it is he*'?" Todd said, when Nellie had hung up.

Nellie rolled her eyes. "I promise you, that is how she talks. The Raggs think they are hot you-know-what. Now: Raymond Sturbridge. Let's go to the Gethsemane website and take a look. I wonder," she added, "what if you decide that you *like* him?"

"Please," Todd groaned. "I'm taking one for the team, not looking for a date." He kissed her. "I have you."

Nellie held up her phone. "Raymond Troutwise Sturbridge, Director of Client Services," she said, "meet Todd Sweeney, Director of Servicing Clients."

"Very droll," said Todd. "He looks like a sort of preacher-accountant."

"Two skills you gotta have to run a place like that."

"Find him on Facebook."

Sturbridge's Facebook page, alas, was locked up, as Nellie put it, "tighter than a nun. But," she said, "we have a name and a time, and we are about to have an ad placed on Ferdslist." Her thumbs went to work. After a minute she turned the phone for Todd to see.

"How come you made me 20?" he asked.

"You'll seem a little more legal."

"Wait? I'm volunteering to let him do *all this* to me?"

"What else? You're not gonna hafta actually *do* it."

"Okay, so, next thing. The, um, 'dimensions' you gave me are a little off. He's gonna wanna see a picture, and even if I did have what you say—"

"Silly! We're using someone else's picture."

"Who?"

"There's a million! Look." She tapped her screen. "Erection Reflection Collection. Selfies of guys naked in bathroom mirrors."

"I guess there really is one born every minute."

"Damn! This one makes my hoo-hoo hurt just to look at. Plus, skeevy. But this one." She tapped. "More wholesome."

"What about the one holding the beer can next to his—?"

"Ta-a-acky-y-y! Likewise, Plaid Shirt here is disqualified. And this one seriously needs to trim his bush—"

"Wait. This one! He's already in a public bathroom, and the lanyard and the ID, like he's kind of official, but still in a T-shirt and the jeans."

"Okey-doke," Nellie said. "So he is now you, and you are now him. Now, the subject line is what? 'Tomorrow afternoon, rest stop off Interstate 69 between'—help me out, map app—'South Hook and Fort Troy,' right? Only the headings are shorter here. How about just, 'Highway Head, I-69 North.'"

"Gross!" Todd said.

"But you're not *doing* anything!" Nellie said.

"Just that there are people in the world who spend so much time on this," Todd said.

"Judg-men-tal!" Nellie sang. "Considering the time you used to spend on video games." She slouched and furiously mimed button-pushing between her legs. "Same thing," she concluded. Todd sighed, took her right hand, and kissed it.

Just how much time a man might spend pursuing another man online, the two friends were about to find out. Back at the Sweeney house, while all three tried to study, Nellie's phone buzzed. Most of the replies she dismissed as "Not Sturbridge," without showing Todd. They managed to keep Toby out of it by making everything sound quiet and casual and just-between-us.

As the sky darkened, suddenly Nellie put down her history notes and slumped, looking pensive and sad.

"What is it, Nells?"

"Kitchen," she said. "Who wants cocoa?"

Toby stuck up his hand, wrapped in a long sleeve. Nellie and Todd went off.

While heating milk, Nellie explained. "Something I kinda haven't been showing you. I hate to say it. It sounds politically incorrect, but it's all so sad." She scrolled on her phone. "One guy e-mailed, like, six times, begging. Most of them are overweight. One guy's wearing panties. I mean, fine. But sending pictures of it to strangers? I guess no one in his real life accepts him in panties. I know I shouldn't say it. I shouldn't judge. But they have wives, most of them." She held up her phone. "A lot of them say so! One of them says he'll come if you can finish by three so he can pick his kids up from school. One of them wanted to *bring* his kid. Wanted to make sure it would be quick and in *your* car, because then he could leave the kid watching a video in *his* car. That's the one who emailed six times. He's going to try one more babysitter, then email again. Some of 'em want to see your butt."

"And?"

"I found a mirror shot from behind. The guy's build pretty much matches the guy whose front we're using."

"Maybe all this isn't such a good idea," Todd fretted.

"Todd, these people have nothing to do with us. It's sad, but they're not our problem." The phone vibrated again. Nellie turned the milk down. "Okay," she said gamely, "this one's age and the build kinda match Sturbridge. Let's ask for a pic."

Mrs. Sweeney came in and volunteered to mix the chocolate. Todd and Nellie adjourned to the pantry.

The gentleman declined to send a picture ("Discretion is a must," he said), but the time he wanted to meet did match the time Sturbridge would be coming to the Raggs'. Then came the clincher. "He'll be 'driving up from St. Joseph'!" Nellie announced. "Where the conversion camp is! Quick: he wants to know more of what you'll do with him."

"Ask his name," Todd said.

"He's not going to give his real name!"

"Not the first time. Just ask."

The answer came back. "Frank," she said.

"Now say, 'Is that really your name? I don't like phonies.'"

102

Nellie typed. A minute later: "Oh, my God!"

"Toldja!"

"His name is Ray! Damn! How did you know?"

"He wants my approval," Todd said.

"Poor guy!"

"That's the way the Oreo crumbles."

"Uh-oh! Ray wants to know your license plate so he'll recognize you."

Todd shook his head. "Just tell him the make and model and that I'll be standing outside it. Tell him there'll be no mistaking me."

Nellie's thumbs worked.

"Oh, by the way," Todd said. "What's my name?" Nellie looked up questioningly. "You know, in this charade."

"'Race.'"

"'*Race*'?"

"It sounds sexy, okay? And I'm giving him your cell number so you two can text."

"Guess I'm all in now."

"Don't forget your paddle."

"'Race.' Damn."

"Kids! Cocoa's ready!"

The world outside had gone completely dark.

CHAPTER TWELVE

*How gratifying it may be for the oppressed to succeed
in altering their natures so as to seem at last to win the
approbation of their oppressors—Yet how great the price
of such self-abnegation, for at his core the oppressor is
unmoved and has even crueler demands in store*

Anthony kind of, well, liked it.

It was different. Powerful. He had thought it impossible. Never even dreamed of it. Standing with his chest out. Speaking louder and deeper. Lifting, carrying, giving orders to other boys and watching them actually obey.

Bates had them cleaning up the yard. They wore jeans, flannel shirts, work boots, and leather gloves. Bates had put Anthony in charge of his own crew. Watching over them, Anthony tried a little swagger. He liked it. His parents, teachers, classmates, even strangers had told him he walked like a girl. Now, well, wait till they saw this!

At first, he had hated Bates for making him behave this way. It wasn't him. But then, maybe it was, a little. He liked feeling what other guys got to feel. What real men felt. He took long strides and swung his arms. "Get these fallen branches over here!" he shouted. "You! Gimme a hand! On the double!" The boy trotted right over. If he dragged his feet, Anthony snapped out, "Let's move it, bud! Don't got all day!" (He knew better, but somehow he found it exciting to say "Don't got.")

After all those years being mocked and beat up and told he was wrong wrong *wrong*, for once now he was right. After being called hopeless, he had hope. Besides, he would soon get out of here and wouldn't need any of this. He could just do a little when he wanted. He wondered if Toby would like it. Quickly he turned away from the thought and hoisted an armful of branches, not caring that a twig scratched his face. He actually made sure it did. Heaving a rock, he watched his forearms work. Then he went for a bigger rock. Bates actually said, "Don't hurt yourself." Anthony pretended not to hear. He couldn't wait to move rocks in front of his parents. His mother would say, "Don't hurt yourself," and he would scowl and ignore her.

And this did mean he could be strong and protective for Toby. But Toby would also have to learn to stand on his own two feet more. Toby was maybe a little like those boys who complained. A bit oversensitive. Anthony decided he could teach Toby to be like this. Just for sometimes. Then Anthony wondered—when he went back, would he have to have a girlfriend? Maybe someone from church? But he and Toby could still be together. They'd figure it out. Somehow.

"You!" Bates called to him. "Come here."

"Yes, sir." As Anthony came up to him, Bates turned on his heel and went inside. Anthony put on his best swagger and followed. He set his face in a frown. He was not afraid. Maybe a bit nervous. Had he failed at something? Was his walk or his voice not quite correct?

Bates motioned Anthony into his office. A single lamp illuminated the desk. Anthony heard whimpering. Bates switched on an overhead light, dim yet somehow over-whelming. Anthony's stomach fell. In the corner, watched by one of Bates's assistants, sat a boy Anthony knew. Joshua. He and Joshua had come here together. They had snuck moments alone to talk about favorite music or movies. The guards caught on and separated them. Still, they gave each other signals in passing. Smiles and winks. Funny faces so quick no one saw.

More recently, though, Anthony found he didn't like it when Joshua dragged his feet during work details. He wanted Joshua to be a little more—okay, "manly." "Normal." Just a bit. What was wrong with that, sometimes? Why couldn't Joshua just do the work? That was a man's attitude.

And couldn't he call himself "Josh," like other guys named "Joshua"? Anthony had started calling himself "Tony."

Joshua was trembling and wiping away tears. Anthony understood, but why did he have to do this in front of *Them*? He tried to beam a thought: *Josh! Stop! Just stop it, Josh!*

"Now, Tony," Bates said, standing legs apart, arms akimbo behind the oaken desk, "we have a problem. With this young man. Whom I think you know."

Anthony hated that he could not stop a gnawing fear in his stomach. He folded his arms and cocked his head, as though to say, "Got it. Go on."

"This young man," Bates continued, "does not think he needs to *participate* as the others do. He does not wish to *do his part.*"

Joshua looked pleadingly at Anthony. Anthony looked away. He observed—thinking maybe this had always annoyed him—that Joshua had a weak chin.

"And I was wondering your opinion."

"My opinion?" said Anthony. "Sir?"

"What is your opinion of the job this young man has been doing?"

Anthony looked at Joshua again. His wide, wet eyes. Softly he said, "Please, Anthony!"

107

Anthony looked away, sick that he had had a momentary thought: *What a pussy! NO!* He must not think that!

Bates came around the desk and placed a hand on Anthony's shoulder. "You've been supervising," he said with a smile. "And doing very well, I might add. Do you think this young man's work has been . . . satisfactory?"

Anthony opened his mouth slowly, then closed it.

"Up to *our standard*," Bates said. "The standard we must meet *as men*. Is that how you would describe this young man's work?"

"Please, Anthony-y-y!"

"Well . . ." Anthony smiled a bit and tried to sound reasonable. "Maybe not quite one hundred percent." He glanced at Bates, then at Joshua, then at Bates again. "But—"

"No?" Bates snapped. He stood frozen.

"Almost!" Anthony said. "And I just think with—"

"His work is not up to standard?"

"Like I said—ahem!—excuse me—maybe not a full one hundred percent. Sir. But with—"

"And tell me, Tony. What happens here when work is not, as you just said yourself, 'Not. Quite. One hundred. Percent'? What can a *real* man expect if his work is 'Not. Quite. One hundred. Percent'?"

"He can expect he has to get better!" Anthony ejaculated confidently.

"Ye-e-es," Bates said, nodding. Anthony exhaled. "But. Perhaps there is something else that he can expect. Something more concrete. Something with a more *measurable* outcome." He paused, then added, "Something that can be . . . *enumerated.*"

Anthony frowned and bit his lip.

Bates sat on the desk and folded his arms. "What would that be, now, Tony?"

Anthony could not help but look—and Bates saw him look—at the collection of paddles, canes, and other implements, set in a perfect row on the wall. As quickly and as smoothly as possible, Anthony looked away. "I'm sorry," Bates said offhandedly. "What were you looking at just now?"

"Sir?"

"Just now. What were you looking at?"

"I, um, don't know, sir."

"At the wall over there?"

"Maybe, sir. I might—"

"Or at something *on* the wall?"

"Sir, there are a few things on that wall, so—"

"And what would those things be? What would there be on my wall that you might have been looking at?"

Bates nodded as Anthony enumerated each thing on the wall: a picture of Jesus, a plaque for Best Corrective Therapy Facility of 2013, another picture of Jesus, another plaque, for 2014, an American flag, and a framed photo of a little blond boy he had seen around. Bates's son, presumably. Finally, Anthony had named everything but the punishment implements. "And what else?" Bates asked abruptly.

"What else? Oh. Well. Of course. Those." He began to point but dropped his hand. He hated himself. He was supposed to be stronger than this.

"'Those'? Tony, I invite you just to step over there and stand in front of 'those.'" Briskly, Anthony did so. "I want you to name 'those.' Left to right."

Anthony took a deep breath. "Um. A paddle. Um, another paddle, um, with holes. A bigger, um, paddle."

"Turn around, Tony."

He turned. Bates took one stride toward him and slapped him across the face. "Say it like a man," he said, and turned away.

Anthony turned back and quickly listed every implement.

"Very good," Bates said. "And why were you looking at those implements?"

Anthony shrugged. "They were in my line of vision. I guess."

Instantly Bates was on him and slapped him again, harder. It stung terribly. "Once more," he said. "Why were you looking at them?"

Looking slightly to one side, so that Joshua would not be in his field of vision, Anthony said, "Because I expect you will use one of them on Josh."

"I see," said Bates.

Anthony could not see Joshua, but he could still hear him whimper.

Stop. Now. Josh!

"What if I told you," Bates asked, "that you were wrong?"

"Sir?"

"That I am not going to use those implements on Josh."

"Oh. Well—"

"You are," Bates said.

A moment of silence. "M-me?"

"Is this how a *man* confronts duty and responsibility?" Bates asked. "'M-m-m-m-m-*meeee*?'" he whined.

Anthony felt dizzy.

"Or," Bates said, lowering a hand onto Anthony's shoulder, "does a *real* man say, 'Yes, sir! Immediately, sir!'?"

Anthony pined to be that "real man." He had thought he finally was. But it was nothing. All the lifting and carrying and gruff talk meant nothing. Bates could crush his dreams of masculinity in no time, right now. Minutes seemed to pass. Men didn't hesitate. They faced what had to be done, however terrible. He had to be realistic. Josh would get it anyway. So, wasn't it his "duty"—?

"Yes, sir!"

There. He'd done it. Maybe this wouldn't be so bad.

"Good," Bates said, expressionless. "And Tony, tell me, how would you, as a dutiful man, propose to punish Josh?"

Anthony knew the answer. Two words with which they

all were threatened every day. But he couldn't say them. He couldn't, just *couldn't* be Bates.

Joshua whimpered, and suddenly Anthony said, "Hard and fast, sir!"

Silence. Except for Joshua's tiny sounds. Anthony glanced at him a half-second, then away, then did a double take. In that half-second their eyes had met. Joshua's mouth had twitched, adorably. Something about boys like that. Like him, like Anthony. A sweetness— *NO!*

"Hard. And fast." Bates's voice sounded dead. Dead as Anthony felt inside. Drained of will. The thing he had foolishly thought was masculinity, gone. His hands tried to make fists. They curled, then went limp. He could barely stand. His eyelids drooped.

"With which instrument," Bates asked, "shall we begin? Tony? A swift decision is required of you. With which instrument shall we begin?" Anthony didn't answer. "Surely you have some idea, *Tony*. If you do not have an idea, you may find I do. And I will not hesitate to try that instrument first on you, so that you may understand its power."

Anthony thrust his finger at the bigger of the paddles with the holes. "That one!" he shouted. He breathed a little easier now. Soon this would be over.

Bates took the paddle down. "This?" Anthony nodded. Bates brought the paddle to Anthony. "Proverbs 13:24" was burned into it. "Take it," Bates said. Anthony did. Bates lay a hand on his shoulder again. "Be a man now," he said, and then he added, "Son."

Anthony felt the weight and solidity of the oak, the *fact* of it. He clutched the handle. The blade jerked upward.

"That's my boy," Bates said. "Now, Tony, you know, if you do not do this job, I will. And to you as well." He unbuttoned his shirt and pulled it off. He flexed his bicep in front of Anthony's face. Muscles and veins popped. "Feel it," he whispered. "I'm not into that anymore," Anthony said stoutly. Bates smiled. "Good. But this one time you have dispensation. Go ahead. Feel." Anthony lifted his hand and ran his fingers over Bates's warm skin, the strangely rock-hard muscle beneath. "Now," Bates said, "you think what that could do with the instrument you're holding. You would not walk straight again. But that won't happen, if you do your job. Hard and fast. Now."

Anthony longed for a moment alone with Joshua to tell him how he really felt and that it was better this way. Surely Joshua understood. In a way, he was being spared.

Bates went to Joshua. "Young man," he said, "remove your trousers."

Even as Joshua undid his belt he whimpered, "Please, sir!" Defeatedly, he removed his trousers.

"Underpants as well," Bates said. Lip trembling, Joshua complied. "Tony," Bates said, "what should Joshua do next?"

Without hesitation but not very loudly, Anthony said, "Assume the position." He went over to Joshua.

Quietly Joshua said, "You're my friend, Anthony."

"It's 'Tony'!" he said, before he could stop himself.

"Good," Bates said.

"Spread 'em," Anthony said, none too convincingly. More than anything, he would remember how compliant Joshua was.

And then there was nothing left but to do it.

The first swat wasn't so bad. Joshua winced a bit. How many would there be? Not enough to *kill* anyone. Okay. Second one, out of the way. But soon Joshua began to break Anthony's heart with his desperate attempts not to shake or to cry. Joshua, too, was trying to "be a man." Anthony felt like less of a man than he had ever felt.

Finally, thirteen. Halfway. If this was Bates's usual twenty-five. What if he wanted more? Anthony looked at him. He did not look back. His face quivered, mouth slightly open, eyes riveted on Joshua's behind. Anthony decided to continue, though Bates, hardly seeming to be there, had given no signal. Anthony delivered the fourteenth stroke and Joshua made a spluttering sound, the gurgling of a suppressed scream or sob. Anthony was horrified to hear himself think, *At least I don't have to feel it.* There was actually something exciting about Joshua's small, pale bottom turning red, then purple, then blistered. Something exciting about his lonely humiliation and fear. About the impact and being the one to control it. Anthony had lost count. Finally, Bates sneered, "What are you trying to do? Kill the kid?" Anthony felt suddenly frustrated. *One more*, he thought. The impact was so satisfying. He gripped the handle. Joshua spluttered and gasped. Bates reached for the paddle. Anthony loosened his grip. His palm was sweating. If only he could sleep.

"What do you think?" Bates rasped. "Has your *friend* learned his lesson?"

Anthony forced himself to nod. Once. Twice. He wished Bates *and* Joshua would both just *STOP!* and let him sleep.

"Really?" Bates said. "Has he really, truly learned?"

Anthony fought to keep his eyes open. The purple patches on Joshua's behind practically bled.

"I don't think he has," Bates breathed. "That type never learns." A pause. "Until they are *mastered*. Do you know what I mean, Tony?"

"No." Sleep, *sleep*.

Bates's hand was on his crotch, massaging.

"There is one instrument here," Bates growled, "more powerful than anything on that wall. Properly applied, it makes a young man acknowledge his subordination." Anthony could feel Bates's hot breath on his ear. "Tony. I want you to use that instrument on this young man." He gave Anthony's crotch a squeeze. "Until you are *satisfied*. Can you do that, Tony?"

The haze cleared just enough for Anthony to say, "No, sir."

A pause.

"Excuse me?" Bates's voice was leaden.

"No. Sir."

Bates withdrew his hand so roughly that Anthony spasmed. "You refuse?"

"Yessir."

"Are you aware," Bates asked, "that, if you are not *up to the job*, someone else is?" Bates clutched his own crotch. "And I assure you," he said, "my instrument is more terrible than yours." He turned to the assistant, who stood in a shadow, looking away. "Fetch a gag," he said.

Anthony experienced a horrible moment of disorientation. Would it be better—? He couldn't! But . . .

"Take that one away!" The assistant leapt at Anthony.

"No! Wait!" Anthony said. Now he was fully awake.

"Away!" Bates bellowed. "Now!"

"I'll do it!" Anthony shouted. "Please!"

"Too late!" Bates said. "But, Tony, there is one last thing you can do, and I might go easier on your friend. You can play a game with me." Bates undid his belt and shucked his shoes, trousers, and undershorts. Anthony could not help but look. What Bates had said about his anatomy was true. "You can help, Tony, with a game called Get the Master Hard. It will spare your friend at least some of his ordeal."

Anthony knelt. He kept his eyes closed, and the entire time he repeated in his head, *I have to, this doesn't count, no one is betraying anyone.*

After little more than a minute, Bates pushed him away. "Don't wanna get me too excited," he said with a smirk. He signaled to the assistant. Then Anthony was in the corridor, roughly conveyed to his cell.

That night, when the silence screamed, Anthony, under his meagre blanket, heard a key in his door.

The door squealed open and thundered shut. And Bates was on him.

When Bates was at last satisfied, he dressed, and then bent down to the shivering, gasping Anthony and said, "You might like to know. I just couldn't spare your friend. The screams were too exciting."

Then the key turned the other way. Silence fell, and it had a melody, a wailing, rising and falling. And that melody had words: "Oh, Toby, I'm so sorry. I'm so, so sorry!"

CHAPTER THIRTEEN

*Our hero meditates on the lives of those whose desires
are satisfied in secret—Not one but two tormented souls
pursue our hero!—He who allows his frustrated desire
to curdle into cruelty shall pay the price—Tobias uncovers
a secret—Our hero pledges to Tobias his love and
protection, yet there are dark intimations—The great
friendship of Tobias and our hero is narrated*

Clouds low. Sky and road gray. Cars swished. On a knoll
above I-69, a low stone bunker. Around it, rows of cars.
People trudged to and from it to relieve themselves.
Change rattled in vending machines. Todd leaned against
his car, trying to look like James Dean. Nellie had found
him a worn leather jacket.

On the other side of the highway, cornfields rolled away
into cold mist. Here and there, little white houses. In some
lived men who felt what Ray Sturbridge felt. They had
wives and children, but secretly, all alone, they dreamed
what Ray dreamed. Some might even have answered
Nellie's ad and never heard back. They sat alone in their
homes and pined for "Race." Maybe they answered other
ads. And never heard back. Or they spent hours or days in
inconclusive exchanges. Maybe they sent a picture. And

the exchange stopped. Or they made appointments—in parks, at one-star motels, at rest areas like this. They made excuses to wives and children. But the other guy didn't show. Or he showed but wouldn't follow through. Went back to his own family. Such dramas were a part of this landscape, as surely as fields and white houses and cars and chill wind. And silence.

Suddenly, coming up to the parking lot, the car they had said Sturbridge would drive! A figure hunched at the wheel stole glances left and right. Todd hooked a thumb in a belt loop and let his fingers fall along the placket of his fly. He scratched his chest lingeringly and stared at the driver, who glanced back at him for just a moment. Maybe Sturbridge, maybe not. He glanced again. No, it had to be.

The car drove all the way to the end of the lot and parked. Its lights went off. Todd waited. The macho pose was getting uncomfortable. The figure in the car stayed perfectly still. Todd strolled into the middle of the lot and craned his neck to see.

The driver's hands were folded under his chin. Was he praying? Shit! He couldn't whack a guy he'd just seen praying! He thought of texting Nellie but decided to wait. Maybe he had the wrong guy. The figure remained immobile.

Then something else caught Todd's eye. Across the way, a strapping man with a shaved head stood by an SUV, sort of tentatively signaling to him. The man's facial expressions were a mixture of pleading, impatience, fear, and desire. Todd's heart thudded. Did he know this guy? Would this ruin the plan?

The man turned and stuck his head into his SUV. Someone was inside. Todd saw the top of a little blond head. A kid! This was the guy who had emailed Nellie (or "Race" or whoever) about 20,000 times, saying he could come have sex while his little boy stayed in the car watching videos. He had come anyway! Todd looked back to the other car.

Sturbridge (or whoever) was getting out. Todd went back to his car and reassumed his macho pose, now very much aware that Dad of the Year was watching, too. Sturbridge came his way. His hat was tipped forward, but the lower half of his face matched the photo online, and his build was slight, almost as though there were nothing under the coat. Todd's heart thumped. How could he possibly eliminate Sturbridge with Dad of the Year lurking? Sturbridge was now just four or five feet away, and . . .

He passed Todd without a look or a word and went into the bunker. Dad of the Year was still pacing and trying to get his attention.

Todd drew himself up, took a few steps toward Dad of the Year, and with a dead-serious look, shook his head firmly. Then he went back to his car. Behind him he heard, "Aw, Jeez! Come on!" He looked back. Dad had retreated to the driver's seat. Todd heard a faint "Daddy! Daddy!" Todd shuddered and looked away, toward the bunker.

Minutes passed. Wind thrummed in his ears. Cars swished. He wanted to text Nellie, but she would just say get on with it. She had not seen the stoop of Sturbridge's shoulder or his ashen face. Someone would miss their dad tonight. Their dad, who made a living torturing helpless kids.

Now Sturbridge came back, head down, hands in pockets. Todd assumed his studly stance. Sturbridge came closer, closer, looked up for a second, a slight twitch of his thin, colorless lips, and kept walking.

"Hey there!" Todd said.

Sturbridge did not break stride, but he flinched.

"Don't I know you?" Todd asked. Oh, great. He had just caused Dad of the Year to look.

Sturbridge stopped but did not turn. He fingered something in his pocket. "Don't know," he said, barely able to gasp the words out.

"I think you want to meet me," Todd said.

Sturbridge's face—impassive, sad, yet somehow rageful—turned for just a second. "Are you—?"

"Race." Todd put out a paw. "Pleased to meet you." Across the way, he heard Dad of the Year say, "Aw, come *on!*" Then the little boy's voice: "Daddy! Come look!" Damn! Dad of the Year had gotten out of his car again. Now he turned back. "Sweet Pie," he said, "just be *quiet* for a second! Daddy's busy."

"I don't normally do this," Sturbridge said, turning more but ignoring Todd's hand.

"That's okay," Todd said. He found himself wanting to reassure Sturbridge. What if Sturbridge was someone's protector, just as he was? He didn't wear a ring. But no matter what, this man would be Toby's persecutor and the persecutor of hundreds of others. Todd grinned crookedly. "First time for everything, huh?"

Sturbridge's eyes cut left-right. "Can we"—he cleared his throat—"just talk?"

"Sure, man." That made Sturbridge smile a little. "Get in, why dontcha?" Todd was still trying to decide if he liked this "Race" who occupied his body. He had begun to envy Race, to idealize and long for him. Race wouldn't harm anyone. Race would give this guy a good time. He'd answer his prayers, not—

After some hesitation, Sturbridge slipped into the front seat. Dad of the Year threw up his hands, threw himself hard back into his driver's seat, and slammed the door. Todd removed his jacket, tossed it in the back seat, and got into his own car, next to Sturbridge. *Chunk!* went his door. "There's a place I have to be," Sturbridge mumbled.

Todd grinned. "I'm sure it can wait a little," he said gently. "So, you like me? You like how I look?" If only he *were* Race. Someone Sturbridge could trust and, well, not *love*, but—

"Sure," Sturbridge said, looking everywhere but at Todd.

Todd held up his arm, pulled the sleeve of his T-shirt up over his shoulder, grinned, and made a muscle. "You like that?"

Sturbridge glanced and nodded.

"Want to touch it?"

Sturbridge froze. Then he looked at the bicep. His eyes were watery, his breath labored. His hand's journey took several seconds. His fingertips were like autumn leaves. He leaned forward and kissed the bulging muscle. He did it again. And again. "Oh!" he whispered. "Oh, oh!" He made a low moan, desiring and despairing, and he touched his crotch. A tear ran down his face. Todd was afraid he would come and run. He removed Sturbridge's hand from his crotch. "Let's make this last, okay?"

Sturbridge nodded. He wiped the tear. "Cold," he said.

Suddenly Todd imagined Sturbridge having a child, too.

Daddy, guess what I did in school today?

"Why don't we get in back? Relax a little?"

"I do have to be somewhere . . ."

Daddy, read to me?

"It won't take long."

Please, Daddy?

"I don't know . . ."

"Want to see my cock?" Todd asked. He hoped those words would make things go his way.

Sturbridge stared up with an expression that said, *More than anything please God does love me after all He's finally proving it and I will finally have what I want!*

Todd smiled. "Get in back."

Sturbridge scrambled out, looked surreptitiously around the parking lot, then pulled open the back door and dove in. "Why is there plastic laid out?" he asked.

"Us bad boys can't mess up Dad's car, can we?" Todd said. He got out and shot a look over at Dad of the Year. Still watching! Damn! He climbed in back and closed the door. "I mean," he said, "when I do it, there's a lot!" Sturbridge's eyes went wide. He reached for Todd's belt buckle. Todd double-checked for the paddle, out of sight on the floor. His fingers itched. Sturbridge whimpered.

"Easy, man," Todd said. "Lie back. Go on. Where is it you're in such a hurry to get to?"

"Just business."

"What kind of business?"

SHIT! Dad of the Year was right at the window, his face all wonder and tragedy. Sturbridge covered his own face.

"Excuse me," Todd said evenly. He took out his phone, got out of the car, and came right at Dad of the Year.

"No no," Dad said. "Please. I only—"

Todd tapped his phone three times, then held it to his ear. "Hi," he said. "I'm at a rest stop off I-69 and I'm being harassed." DOTY backed away, making pleading motions. "I'm going to give you the license plate." Behind him he heard the other back door open. He turned and held a forbidding hand out to Sturbridge. Remarkably, Sturbridge retreated into the back seat and closed the door again.

Dad ran for his SUV, leapt into the driver's seat, and, accompanied by a cry of "Daddy! You said we'd get Oreos," wrenched the wheel and screeched away.

Todd got back in his car. "I think I might know him," Sturbridge said, gasping. "Goodness, I hope he didn't see me."

"He wasn't looking at you," Todd said coolly. "Now, you want my cock or not? I'm tellin' you, there's gonna be a lot." No. Race wouldn't be that crude.

"Has to be quick," Sturbridge said, checking his watch. "May I make a phone call first?"

"After," Todd said. "You were telling me what business you're in—?"

"What?" He went for Todd's zipper. "I'm, uh, in education."

Todd's entire body clenched. He put his hand over Sturbridge's hand and quickly surveyed the parking lot one last time. Sturbridge looked up. Todd nailed his wet, frightened eyes. "Don't you mean '*re*-education'?" he said icily.

Sturbridge gasped. Going for the door, he mussed the plastic. The paddle came down, edge first—one! two! three! four! five! six! times.

Sturbridge's head lolled. Blood trailed from his mouth. But his eyes were still alive. Todd closed his own eyes and brought the paddle down one more time.

When he opened his eyes, Sturbridge lay dead.

Todd stashed the paddle, pulled out a tissue, and with it plucked Sturbridge's cell phone from his pocket. He quickly wrapped the corpse in the plastic. His hands shook. Toby was safe now. At least they'd bought time.

Exhilarated yet exhausted, he went to pee, then bought a coffee and a granola bar from the vending machines. He texted Nellie a "thumbs up" emoji. She replied with a smiling emoji and "XO CU soon."

Todd strolled down to Sturbridge's car. The light was fading. He memorized Sturbridge's license plate, then returned to his car. Tissue in hand, using Sturbridge's phone, he created a sex ad called "Rest Area I-69." It told what Sturbridge dreamed of getting from a young man, and it ended with, "I'm in the car with license plate . . ." Todd filled it in and posted it. Then he hurled the cell into the woods.

Driving north in the dark he thought of the children whose daddy would not come home that night. Maybe they'd be better off. Maybe their mom would marry another guy just as bad. Lights came on across the fields. Children waiting. Dads reading to them while dreaming of "Race." Tucking them in, telling their wives, "I need some air. Don't wait up."

Such men were not his worry. Nor was the (deserving) corpse in the back seat. His concern was Toby and all the boys like him. He had given those boys time.

He reached Nellie as the moon rose. They hauled Sturbridge up to the bakehouse. "This is disappointing!" Nellie said, when they stretched him out on the floor.

"I know," Todd said. "When I saw him I thought, *Fifteen pounds, max.*"

"I could make some cheese, too," Nellie suggested.

"It's not the same if people have a choice."

"I know. But there's that four-cheese idea you had. It's brilliant." She kissed his cheek. "People love that. I vote for ricotta, fontina, mozzarella, and Parmesan." They stripped and made love over Sturbridge's twisted form, and then quickly, naked, went to work.

"By the way," Nellie said. "Remember the guy with the little kid who emailed six times?"

"Yeah?" What had Dad of the Year done? Had he stayed? Had he seen something?

"He emailed about ten more times saying he was right there and why didn't you pay attention to him?"

Todd was about to explain when there came a rumbling and thudding against the side of the garage. Their eyes met. They covered themselves. Too late they realized someone was coming up the stairs, fast. Their eyes went to the door. Unlatched! How had they not—?

Nellie dove for the light switch. The bulb over the table went out. The door flew open.

"Toby!"

"Hey, you guys'll never guess! That counselor from—" He stopped. Todd, clutching his T-shirt in front of himself, stepped up to block the view of the corpse. "Oh," Toby said.

"Tobes, it's okay," Todd said.

Toby backed out. "Guess I interrupted something." He looked at Nellie. "Your mom said I could— I'm sorry!" The light over the door illuminated his horrified face.

"Tobes," Todd said. "Wait!"

He turned and they heard him going down the stairs. Todd rushed to dress. "What are you doing?" Nellie asked, her voice breaking.

"I don't know," Todd said. He began to cry himself. Once dressed he stumbled onto the landing. Toby was gone.

Todd leapt down the stairs and broke into a run. On the

street he spotted Toby, running clumsily and exhaustedly. He ran after him.

Toby turned. "No, Todd!" he wept. "Please!"

Todd threw his arms around him. "No, Todd, no!" Toby bawled. "Please! No!"

"We're gonna talk," Todd said. He pulled Toby across the street and into the woods.

"I can't!" Toby sobbed. "Todd, what did you do?"

Todd pulled him along, panting, until they came to a fallen tree. The only sounds were crickets and leaves above. Todd sat Toby next to him and hugged him to his chest.

"I'm so sorry, Tobes," he said. "I didn't mean—"

"No, Todd, no," Toby whimpered.

"Toby, I only wanted to protect you."

"I know," came the miserable answer.

"I only wanted you to be safe and love Anthony and grow up and be free of these terrible people, of all of it, and be a big, strong, handsome man and get married and have a bunch of kids as sweet as you are and live in a house with a garden and I swear that's all I ever wanted, Tobes."

"I know, Todd—"

"But Tobes, the more awful people are, the more powerful they are. Maybe God and my mom forgive them, but I don't. God doesn't have to get up every day and worry how these people are going to ruin His life. He looks down and says, 'Oops, I made a psychopath. Oh, well.' But we're the victims. And I swore I would protect you, buddy. I swore on my dad's grave—"

"I know," Toby snuffled sweetly.

"I swore I would protect you and my mom and Nells and everyone. That's what a man does. But some people still get away with anything. Anyone in any position of power is sick. That's how they're there. Their sickness. Year after year they lord it over the rest of us, till we're finally dead. And they get awards and promotions, and God says to us, 'Welcome to Heaven. Sorry you had to be destroyed by a fellow human being. I understand the pain, but suicide's a sin, so off to Hell with you. I know your parents threw you out and they beat you up at school and they wouldn't even let you have a wedding cake, but it's off to the flames!'"

"Todd, it's okay," Toby whimpered.

Wiping away tears, Todd asked, "What's okay, Toby? What's okay about any of this?"

"I know you were just trying to help me," Toby said.

"Oh, Tobes!"

"I know you wanted to protect me and give me good things. You hate anyone who does anything bad to me or your mom or other people. It's okay. I'm sorry I interrupted you guys."

"No, Toby!"

"You were trying to protect Anthony, too. That's good enough for me. I won't tell. I don't even know what I'd tell them! And the same goes for Nellie. You love Nellie, don't you?"

Todd nodded. "Yes."

"Then you have to protect her, too. You're right, Todd. There are bad people out there. I just want you to do one thing for me, Todd. Just one more thing."

"What?"

"Help Anthony. Please, Todd! It's getting worse and worse for him. He was supposed to get out last week, but they didn't let him. We write each other in code. We use acrostics, y'know? Where the first letter of every line adds up? He tells me how much he hates it there. I'm afraid he's going to lose it. Or try to escape, and they do terrible things to kids who escape. He could end up there forever. I don't know what I'd do. I can't sleep, I can't eat—"

"We'll fix it, Tobes—"

"It has to be soon! Before Gethsamane sends someone else for me. They're worried about that guy they sent. They found his car abandoned in a rest stop, but no one knows anything else. It weirded my parents out. For a second they sort of reconsidered. But they'll get over it, and the camp will send a new guy. If we can save Anthony, then he and I can get away from all this."

"We'll find a way, Tobes," Todd said stoutly. "Don't you worry." He rocked the boy. "I promise. On my dad's grave."

"Todd, you're so good to me."

"I love you, Tobes."

"I love you, too, Todd. If I can ever do anything for you, you let me know. I don't know what it could be, but the minute there is something, you tell me."

"I will, Tobes."

"Promise? Not, like, yeah, whatever, but really."

"You can count on it, Tobes. Hey, listen. Toby?"

"Yeah?"

"If ever I— If I ever had to, like, go away, for a while—?"

"What?"

"I'm not saying I will. And we'll make sure Anthony's safe. But after that, I might . . . for a little while—"

"Could I come with you?"

Tears filled Todd's eyes. "I love you enough," he said, "to say no. We'll get Anthony back. Then after that, maybe, for a little bit, you can't be mixed up with me."

"Can I text you and stuff?"

"We'll see," Todd said, though he already knew the answer was no.

"Walk you back to Nellie's?" Toby said.

"I think you should go home and sit tight," Todd said. "And let me know if the conversion place sends anyone else."

They walked out of the woods holding each other close. Up at the road the boys gave each other final hugs and kisses; then they broke and went in opposite directions.

The next day, after Nellie's history test, she and Todd drove up to the state capital and gave Mrs. Plouf's eight dollars to Congregation Beth Ahm, to help pay for Spanish classes for social workers. After, at the top of the synagogue steps, Nellie sighed and said, "It just kills me that she doesn't *know*."

"Fosho," Todd sighed. He took her hand and they went down.

The next night, after Raymond Sturbridge had yielded a disappointing "fourteen pounds of product," as Nellie put it, the two made love on the table, then lay there naked and talked business. They had set the liver aside as always, but Nellie had not been pleased with her pâté recipe. "I think freeze-dried peppercorns are the way to go," she said. "Next time."

Todd silently wondered if there would be a next time. "Ryan Plouf's liver turned out fine," he said.

"His mother liked it," said Nellie, "but she would." She turned and propped herself up with one arm. "So tell me something."

"Yes, ma'am?"

"Toby."

"Toby?"

"What, when, where, why, and how? I mean, a straight guy and a gay guy being such best buds—"

"I dunno. We were so young it seemed, like, natural. We were four–five years old. Me five, him four. Our parents were friends. His folks were sane then. My dad was alive." Nellie snuggled closer. "Everyone was at our house one night, and Tobes fell asleep. It was winter. They just put him in bed with me. When he woke up in the morning he was happy 'cause my mom makes this French toast he loves. After that we did it a lot. It felt good. Neither of us had any brothers. By the time we were, like, eleven or twelve, well—"

"Puberty interfered?" Nellie said. "Right?"

"What do you mean?"

"He liked guys. You didn't. Wasn't it confusing for him?"

"No. He talked to me first of anyone. About 'feeling different.'" Todd smiled. "That's what he called it. I told him he was perfect, and that's why he was my friend. Then he started to hear terminology. So he's asking me, 'What's this? Why's that?' Then his parents joined Blessed Beams of Light. He brought me these brochures and he cried. He's in tears. *Tears*. Asking me please *please* not to think he'd ever look at me 'that way.' I said, 'And what if I did think that? I'd just have to say, "Tobes, we are brothers. We've gone far down the road of one kind of love. It kind of can't be any other way."' And I said I was proud to have a brother like him. And we went on, you know, cuddling up. Like always."

Nellie grinned. "What about, um, 'morning wood'?"

Todd grinned. "What about it?"

"Didn't you two ever—?"

"Well, we *were* teenagers!" Todd said. He turned to face her and gently brushed his knuckles over her breast. "First time I woke up with him and with a boner, I didn't think about it, like, in relation to him. I did think it'd be weird to spoon him with it, though. So I went to the bathroom. There was a mirror on the back of the door. I stripped and looked at myself, standing at attention. And what I thought of was my dad."

Nellie raised an eyebrow. She took his hand, placed it on her breast, and held it there.

"I thought what a good man he was and how he had protected us all those years. And I saw myself in the mirror, hard, and I thought: that's what a boner means. Beyond the obvious. It's a reminder to a guy that he's a defender. So I put my underwear on again and went back to bed without doing anything. I lay there, and I swore to myself that I would be Toby's protector, always. After that, whenever I woke up hard, that's how I understood it. A reminder that I had a duty to people in my life." Nellie caressed the center of Todd's naked torso gently, up and down. Todd grinned. "Not that we didn't have our moments."

"Moments?"

"Once in a while we'd, y'know, 'rub one out.' Guys do. Brothers actually do, sometimes, so that was kinda where my argument broke down. Then he met Anthony, so—"

Nellie let her hand stray down. She kissed him tenderly. "Will you be my protector?" she whispered.

He slipped his hand around her back. "I already am." He pressed his mouth to hers.

"So what was it like?"

"What was what like?"

"When you 'rubbed one out.'"

"Nice. We'd get side by side, and we were shy at first, about, like, wanking with each other. But you can't control—"

"But you sure like girls, too!"

Todd scowled. "Of course I do! It's not mutually exclusive. I like what I have with men, when I have it."

"So . . . you'd call yourself bi?"

He grinned. "'Androphile,' maybe. Facebook's got fifty-something categories. That should be one of 'em. Anyway, I knew Tobes was a little different from me, but so what? He told me about Anthony without, like, batting an eye."

"That's nice," Nellie said, her nail playing with Todd's chest hair. Then, with what Todd thought was an unusual sadness in her voice, she added, "You are what I wish the whole world was like."

CHAPTER FOURTEEN

Communication from Anthony—A most inconvenient
discovery—Officer Littey deceived, yet for how long?—
A plot is hatched and a mother is left to wonder—
Disguised and under cover of night, our friends
embark on a most urgent mission of rescue

"Look!" Toby said tearfully, holding out a sheet of paper.
"He's going to do something desperate!"

He and Todd huddled on the faded sofa on the Sweeneys'
back porch. A chilly October Saturday faded. Mr. Sturbridge
had sold out that morning, along with Todd's four-cheese
empanadas and a small batch of pâté. Their sign now said
"locally sourced" and "artisanal," but Todd had drawn the
line when Nellie wanted to add, "farm to table."

Todd took the letter from Toby.

It was brief and strangely worded, written by someone
on the edge. Anthony did not say what had happened. He
reported the weather and a few work details. "But look at
the acrostic," Toby said. "Read the first letter of each line
and the last letter."

"'It's Bates,'" Todd read. "'I can't . . . take it . . . anymore.'"

"Bates is the warden or whatever. He's awful. He's in
every letter."

"Let's think about this," Todd said. He felt his chest constricting. Something happening to Anthony was as bad as something happening to Toby.

"If he gives up hope!" Toby whimpered. "Then what?"

"We'll bust him out," Todd said, staring at yellow leaves touching down on his mother's hydrangeas.

"How? They have barbed wire and dogs and stuff. And his parents won't do anything. They think nothing bad happens in a place that's 'Christian.'"

"Well," Todd said, smiling, "then we will address this Bates as the good Christian man he is."

"What?"

Todd texted Nellie two words: "Road trip!"

Nellie texted back: "*Où et pourquoi?*"

"*Le Mouton Soumis,*" Todd replied. "*Déguisés. Comprenez?*"

Nellie sent back a thumbs-up and, "*Nous sommes vraiment trop forts.*"

"I don't see how," Toby complained. "We're kids! And you said it yourself. They always win."

"Yeah, but now I'm going to say something else. I am going to say, no matter how hopeless a situation is, no matter how oppressed you feel, if you act out of love, you win. Nellie and I are gonna act out of our love for you and Anthony."

"Oh, Todd!" The boy clutched him. "I know. But you're not gonna—?"

"We're gonna do whatever to get the two of you back together. They are not winning this time."

The boys huddled in the chilly, darkening air. Suddenly headlights swept the yard. "Nells!" Todd called.

When she got out, she was not in the kick-ass mood conveyed by her texts. "Toby, honey," she said, "I have to talk to Todd alone for a second."

Toby went in to Mrs. Sweeney, who was making tea. Nellie sat down hard on the old sofa. "As I was leaving to come over here, Littey came by."

"And?"

"Remember he bought an empanada this morning? A *Mr. Sturbridge* empanada?"

"Uh-oh!" Todd sighed. "I knew we shoulda made him take the four-cheese!"

"He found," Nellie continued, "something in it."

"'Something'? What?"

"A staple."

"A staple."

"Not a *staple* staple, Honey Muffin. A *surgical* staple."

"They still use those? I thought—"

"Sturbridge is old!" Nellie cried. "I mean, he *was* old. And at some point *in the past* he had surgery, and Dr. Jerk-Off Douche-Nozzle left a staple in him, and it turned up in Officer Littey's empanada! So now he's asking me where I get my meat!"

Todd grinned. "I do hope my name came up!"

"Hardy-har-har! I said I couldn't remember. I ended up naming, like, five places. I had to. And now he's going to check them all! It's just a matter of time—"

"So? He checks them, they say, 'Gee, I have no idea.' Just because it's a surgical staple doesn't mean the meat's human. It could've gotten there any number of ways."

"Name two."

"Butcher with a staple fetish! How should I know?"

"And that's not all."

"Great!"

"He keeps asking about Massauga. Like he knows some-thing and he's not telling. You know how on *Law and Order* they keep saying, 'One more thing,' till the story collapses? I think he's laying a trap. Someone saw us or the car, and he's not saying."

"If someone saw us, why wouldn't he just say so?"

"To make us say it first! He just keeps bringing it up. He almost tripped me up on the timing. I had to pretend my memory wasn't clear because I was so horny for you!"

133

"Works for me!" Todd said. He put his arms around her. She looked adorable in distress. "Look, Nells, I'm sorry I can't be all in knots about this right now—"

"I get it. It's probably good that you—"

"—but we've got maybe a bigger problem."

"The Bending Sheep."

Todd held up Anthony's letter. "Anthony's, like, at the end of his rope. And there's an acrostic. See?" Todd's finger traced the letters. "We think 'Bates' is some sadistic guard. 'I can't take it anymore.' We've got to get him out. I already promised Tobes."

"Okay. I just feel so helpless and stupid. I can butcher an adult human being and make two hundred empanadas from it. From him. But I can't think how to bust someone out of gay conversion camp."

"Nells, what did you tell me junior year, when I didn't want to take Advanced Poetry Seminar?"

"I told you to stretch yourself. Take a leap and trust."

"Well, same here. Couple of weeks ago you wouldn't have thought you could turn Ryan Plouf into a pile of empanadas. But you did. And they sold out. And the pâté."

Nellie nodded. "The Ryan Plouf pâté was good," she said. "The lemon pepper was genius. But I still say frozen peppercorns would be—"

"And we didn't think we could get Sturbridge," Todd said, "but we did. And we can do this." He pulled her closer. "*We* can. Together."

"What if Littey is on our tail?" Nellie asked.

"We'll deal with that, too. Together." He kissed her. "You're my hero," he said. "No matter what happens, you know how to deal with it."

She clung to Todd and spoke into his chest. "If they find us out, though, I won't know what to do."

With remarkably good timing, another set of headlights swept the darkening yard. A police cruiser pulled up behind Nellie's car. "Oh, God!" Nellie gasped.

"Stay cool," Todd said.

Officer Littey stepped out of the car, adjusting his holster.

Mrs. Sweeney appeared. "What's going on?" she asked. Toby stood behind her, nibbling a biscuit.

"Nothing to worry about, ma'am," Littey said. "I just need to speak to this young lady here."

"Nellie?" Mrs. Sweeney asked. "What on earth for?"

"You can go back in the house, ma'am," Littey said.

"Is that an order?"

"I just need to ask the young lady a few questions. Shouldn't take long. If she cooperates."

"Well," Mrs. Sweeney said, "I'll be right here watching. Toby, dear, put on some more water for us." Toby ducked inside.

"What is it, Officer?" Todd asked nonchalantly as the back door swung shut.

"Well," Littey said, swaggering forward, doing his best to sound on top of things. "It's about this business of the staple in the pie." He hooked a thumb in his belt and narrowed his eyes at Nellie. "You gave me the names of some, uh, meat vendors. And I showed your picture around. And some of 'em knew you. Said you used to come in, but it's been a few weeks."

"It certainly has!" Nellie said.

"Huh?" said Littey.

"I am never patronizing the Beef Whistle again!" Nellie snapped. "Or Meat Curtains."

"Well, wait—"

"But that doesn't mean I don't still have their product," she continued. "I bought ahead and froze a ton." She shrugged. "At this point, who knows what came from where? And Todd bought some of it. Honey," she said musically, turning to Todd, "do you remember where you got the meat for today's batch?"

Todd feigned great annoyance. "Are you kidding?" he said. "You send me one place for meat, some other place for flour." He gave Littey a grin. "Bro," he said, "you would not believe how picky she is about butter!"

"Very picky," Nellie cooed, low, with a smirk, "about *butter*." Littey looked flustered. "Say, if we find out who sold me the meat with the staple, can I sue?"

"Look, dude," Todd said, coming over to Littey. "I think I know what's eating you. So to speak."

"And what would that be?" Littey asked.

"First of all," Todd said. "You're thinking about my girl-friend in connection with butter, and that's gotta stop."

"What? Oh. No problem," Littey said manfully.

"Second, you found a surgical staple in an empanada."

"Right! I—"

"Dude," Todd interrupted, "your eyes are telling me you're still thinking about my girlfriend and butter."

"Nope!" Littey said. "Not at all!"

"Okay, so, you find this staple in this empanada. What's the first thing that comes to mind?"

Littey shrugged. "I guess I would call that unusual, wouldn't you?"

"The first thought that would come to *my* mind," Todd said, "is, *'Zounds, this is ground-up human!*"

"No!" Littey said. "Oh, my God! That's disgusting!"

"Right," Todd said. "It's ridiculous. You know it and I know it. But a teeny, tiny part of your cerebellum can't help but think, *Gee willikers, I just ate some muchacho's pancreas!*"

Littey held his hands out pleadingly to Nellie. "Ma'am, I am *not* saying that!" He took out his pad. "Now," he said to Todd, "you mentioned 'Sarah Belle' someone—?"

"Or you bit into some guy's yogurt launcher," Todd continued.

"No!" Littey fairly shouted. "Ab-so-lute-ly not!"

Mrs. Sweeney reappeared. "Is this still going on?" she wanted to know.

"Just wrapping up, ma'am," Littey said. He was holding his stomach and looked a little green.

"I don't know why this was necessary in the first place," Mrs. Sweeney complained, on the edge of tears. "These are two of the hardest-working, nicest, best students at Fleet High, and you just can't keep yourself from coming around making insinuations. This is harassment, and there must be someone I can complain to."

"Not necessary, ma'am," Littey said, putting up his hands and backing away. "I think we have everything cleared up for now."

"Well, I should hope so!"

"I'm just making the point," Todd said, following Littey, "that once you get that idea in your head, you know"—he lowered his voice—"about the meat, it distracts you from the real issue. You suddenly can't stop thinking how some places use pig rectums for calamari—"

"Oh, God, stop!" Littey moaned.

"—when you should be asking, like, are these disappearances connected? Who hated both Squeers and Ryan Plouf? Who would benefit if they disappeared? Don't you watch *Law and Order*?"

"My, uh, favorite, uh, show," Littey moaned.

"Right," Todd said. "That's kinda sad, actually. But anyway, you would know, then, that Lennie Briscoe would never let himself be distracted by thoughts like, *Do they really triple-wash those pig rectums? And if so, in what?* Lennie would—"

With a groan, Littey threw up on what was left of Mrs. Sweeney's Golden Celebration roses.

"It's unprofessional, man," Todd continued. "I'm embarrassed for you."

Littey groaned.

"Because, Officer Littey," Todd continued sympathetically, "you're a good guy. You deserve to do well and get promotions and so forth. But take a freakin' *staple* to your superiors? Next thing, you'll be rounding up stray dogs!"

Littey wiped his mouth. He forced himself to stand and he turned to Todd, his face hardened. In a hoarse voice he snarled, "You listen, Sweeney. You think you're smart, with your frat-boy jokes. I know you two know stuff. You know where Ryan Plouf is. Squeers, too. I ain't told you everything we know on the force. About the staple, or Massauga, or some other stuff. We don't have enough to pull you in yet, buddy, but we're getting close. Unless, of course, you want to make a full confession right now?" When Todd scoffed Littey sneered, "Then I'll be seeing you again, pal. Very soon."

Still gasping and wiping his chin on his sleeve he yanked open the door to his cruiser, swung in, and was gone.

Todd tried to swagger back to where his mother, Nellie, and Toby waited, shivering and wide-eyed on the back porch.

"What did he say?" Nellie asked breathlessly. "And why was he horking on your mother's Golden Celebrations?"

"Todd," said his mother, "should we get a lawyer?"

This question struck Todd to the heart. His mother couldn't afford a lawyer! She shouldn't have to. If her son had created a situation where she even had to *think* about that, then he was the worst son on Earth. He swallowed hard. "No," he said, but his mind raced. What more did Littey know? Was he bluffing because Todd had embarrassed him? A sudden gust blew dry leaves around the driveway.

"Well," Mrs. Sweeey said, pulling her sweater around her, "my mac and cheese is almost done. Why don't you all come in."

They gathered nervously around the kitchen table. It was Todd who finally broke the silence. "Mom, us three are gonna hafta go out tonight," he began.

Mrs. Sweeney's fork stopped. "To a movie?" she asked, trying to sound upbeat.

"Just a little shopping," Todd assured her.

"For what?" When Todd hesitated she put down her fork and, her hands worrying her napkin, she asked them both, "Is there something I should be afraid of?" Toby stared at them. "I know you kids study hard," Mrs. Sweeney said beseechingly. "You work for charity, and Todd, you've been such a friend to Toby. But these past few weeks, you're out late, doing this, doing that. I don't see you. I thought when you came back you'd spend more time here. It's wonderful that you're with Nellie. It's great you two kids found each other. But when I suggest you bring her over, you're too busy. You come home at midnight and study till two a.m. And now I have police coming around. I think I have a right—"

"Mom, it's nothing!" Todd protested.

"It is *something!*" Mrs. Sweeney insisted. "I don't say you're guilty of anything. But there is something going on that shouldn't be." She began to cry. "Todd, I don't know what I'll do if they take you away again. I won't survive!"

"Mom," Todd said, rising and going to her, "I am not going anywhere!"

"She's right, Todd," Toby said tremulously. "The past few weeks there's been all these secrets. And I told you, I don't mind anything you do to try and help me, but—"

"What's he talking about?" Mrs. Sweeney said. "How are you helping him? Does it have to do with that man, Squeers?"

"No!" Todd and Nellie said at once.

"Mom, I'm not going to let anything happen to you or to anyone," Todd pleaded. "Things have been tough this semester. We've been working hard, like you say. And if Squeers is really gone, which we don't know he is, that's good, right?"

"Then there was that boy—" Mrs. Sweeney fretted, wringing her napkin.

"Another bad apple," said Nellie.

139

"That 'bad apple' was someone's son!" Mrs. Sweeney said, suddenly clutching at Todd. Todd thought, *If only she knew*. And he thought, *That's just it. She doesn't know. She has no idea what people will do. Even Squeers. She would never call him what he really is. She lives in a fantasy*. At the same time he hated how cold he sounded. There was just no way to tell his mother what really went on.

He knelt by her chair and tried to tell her that all would be well. Tonight, they were just going on a little shopping trip. They would be right back.

As they put on their coats, Todd fought back tears. He might never see his mother again, might never again hold her and sit and talk to her. If Littey did know something, then who knew what they might have to do, where they might have to go, when they would ever be able to come back? He might not even be able to write her. Nothing that would implicate her or that she would have to lie about.

"We'll be right back," he repeated, and Mrs. Sweeney nodded and tried to smile.

Toby, who had hung back, brooding, until now, stepped forward and said in a clear voice, "Promise. Hey, would I lie to my second mom?"

"No no," Mrs. Sweeney said. "Of course not." She cheered up a little, but in the end, Todd's last image of his mother was a frightened face, huddled in a doorway, shivering, trying to smile, but about to be alone. Again. Perhaps forever.

The door closed. The kids were gone in the dark.

At first they drove in silence. Then Nellie said, "Um, where are we going?"

"Party Hearty." Todd sniffled. "In Gerberville."

"What for?" Toby said.

"Costumes. I have an idea."

"If I'd known," Nellie said, "I would've brought makeup."

"Won't need it," Todd said, smiling through his tears. "Believe me."

"Todd?" Toby said. "What your mom said—"

"Let's not talk about that."

Toby reached into the front seat and took Todd's hand. "I just wish there was some way—"

"What?"

"Well, you don't want to talk about it." A pause. "Some way we could put her at ease." Todd realized that Toby didn't know they would not come back. The Raggs would have to think what they would. He signaled a turn. Nellie said, "This isn't the way to Gerberville."

"One quick stop first," Todd said. "Then we're off."

Nellie stared ahead. Toby hunkered down in back.

They went through town, down under the railroad bridge, and clattered across the river. The church rose. Todd pulled into the parking lot. The headlights shone on the grass and stones, making long shadows.

"I'll just be a second," Todd said.

Toby started to get out, too. Todd put a hand on his shoulder.

"No, Tobes. This has to be just me this time. I'll tell him you said hi, though." And he got out and ran, dancing in the brilliant, fading light. Nellie and Toby sat and fidgeted.

At the back of the cemetery Todd knelt in the dark and felt the stone letters.

"I don't have a lot of time, Dad," he said. "I just came to say I am so sorry, Dad. All I wanted was to protect my friends. But sometimes it's like you're in quicksand and there's no way out, except to do something you wouldn't normally do. Toby's in love, and he deserves to be happy. Maybe I'm going down for it, but a true love will be saved. I love Nellie, too. Maybe we'll go down together. Maybe I'll see you sooner than I think, Dad. If I do, I hope you'll hold me and forgive me. You'll know I did what I thought I had to, to protect Mom and Toby. You told me once that when

141

people were bad, you meet them with your goodness. But there are people you can't do that with. I gotta go, Dad. Just know I love you and Mom loves you, and if I see you, well, we'll hope I won't." He kissed the stone. Then he leapt up and was on his way.

They stood in a brightly lit aisle at Party Hearty. Nellie stared up at rows of black costumes. "A nun," she repeated.

"It's brilliant," Todd insisted.

"A nun."

"You'll talk to Bates as a fellow Christian. You'll say it's for the good of Anthony's soul, or whatever a nun would say. How can he say no?"

"Like this," said Nellie. "'No!'"

"It's our best shot. You think we can just show up as ourselves?"

"And what will you go as?"

"A monk. I mean, duh."

"Do they have monk costumes?"

A pear-shaped young man with jowls, dressed in black, with an unkempt mat of hair and an overbite, waddled up to them. His name tag said, "Hi, I'm BUMP. Ask me how to Party Hearty."

"Um, excuse me, Bump?" Todd said. Nellie smiled. Toby looked worried. "Do you have any costumes for monks?"

Bump frowned and said, "For what?"

"Monks. You know. Brothers."

Still, nothing.

"The male equivalent of nuns!" Toby said.

Bump's eyes went wide. "Male nuns?" he gasped. "That's disgusting! That's a sin!"

"Not male nuns, *exactly*," Todd explained.

"Sir," Bump said, backing away, "no disrespect, but you must be doing the work of Satan."

"Well, that's open to interpreta—" Nellie socked him discreetly on the arm. "Um, that is," he said. "Okay, here's the deal. You've got your nun costumes, right? For the ladies. In the convent. But then you've got also, you know, like, your guys. Dudes. Over in the um, monk . . . er . . . ary . . . ?"

"Monastery," Nellie chirped.

"Monastery!" said Todd. "Sorry. Slept through Renaissance History."

But Bump had fallen to his knees and was rocking back and forth and praying. His jowls quivered. Todd turned to Nellie. "I keep coming up against this," he said.

"Cast these demons from my place of business, Lord," Bump said, breathing hard, "and consign them to the everlasting fire!"

Nellie sighed and entered into her phone a URL from the nun costume package. "They don't make monk costumes," she reported, "but they make priest costumes." She looked up and scanned the rack. "Do we see a priest here?"

Bump continued to pray. He was now sweating. Toby vanished and reappeared with a mousy young woman with teased hair. Her name was Clystine Jo. She informed the trio that, alas, they were out of priest costumes. "So," Nellie returned, "what's the biggest size nun costume you've got?"

"Oh, no!" said Todd.

"I see!" said Nellie. "Now the wimple's on the other head."

"A nun with my build and voice?" Todd demanded.

"You will be mute," said Nellie. "Which will help in a few ways." She held a size 20 nun costume up next to him and shook her head. Clystine Jo dug for a size 22. Meanwhile Nellie picked out a size 8 for herself. "You better be right about this," she muttered to Todd. "By the way, ideally, a habit does not work with the shoes I'm wearing." Clystine Jo found a size 22, and it seemed to fit Todd's build.

They took everything up front. Clystine Jo rang up the costumes while Bump continued to sway and beg to be saved from "transsexual demons."

143

"Doesn't he cut into your earning potential?" Nellie asked.

"Huh?" said Clystine Jo. "Oh, that's just Bump."

"Words for the ages," said Todd.

"Would you like your receipt?" Clystine Jo asked.

Nellie turned to Todd. "We're not deducting this, are we?" she asked. He looked at her sadly.

In the shadowy parking lot, they stuffed their purchases into the back of the car. Then Todd's phone went off.

"Arggh!" Todd punched the side of the car. "Littey came back to the house. Mom's asking what I know about some incident out on the interstate."

"You know nothing," Nellie said crisply.

"Okay, everyone," Todd said. "Change of plan. We're going straight to the Bending Sheep. We'll stop and sleep on the way."

"They have your license plate number," Nellie pointed out. Toby nestled up to Todd, shivering.

"So," Todd said, "we're finding some place with mud or dust to obscure the plate. Everybody in!" They piled into the car.

"Not Massauga!" Nellie said.

"No," said Todd. "The wildlife refuge at Lake Oriemus. Put it in the GPS."

"The GPS can be tracked."

"Then just go. Till we end up some place no one else has gone."

A couple of hours later the car, smeared with dust and mud, sat at the end of the parking lot of a tiny brick church amidst the cornfields. One of them would stay up while the others slept; then they'd switch.

"Wait," Nellie said. "We should be in our costumes."

"Why?"

"If someone comes."

They pulled the costumes out of the back and began changing.

"How come I don't get a costume?" Toby fretted.

"You don't need one," Todd said. "You are playing you. Let us do the talking."

"I am the one who talks!" said Nellie. Todd rolled his eyes and pulled his size 22 habit on.

"And you're sure this will get Anthony out?" Toby asked.

"Yes," said Todd. "When they hear the story that we, that *Nellie* has to tell, they'll be totally cowed and they'll let him go. So long as we don't let them think too much about it."

"I've just got to think what that story is," Nellie sighed.

Soon, Toby was snuggled in back under a blanket. Two nuns huddled in the front, holding hands. They exchanged ideas about what to tell Bates. They decided Todd would stay awake the first shift.

Toby stirred. "Guys?" he said. "I'm scared. I'm sorry."

"Don't be sorry, Tobes," Nellie said. "We're all scared. Just remember: we're doing this for love. And love will triumph."

Nellie squeezed his hand, and he squeezed back.

After another long moment, Toby said, "Todd?"

"Yo!"

"I'm still scared."

Softly Nellie began to sing,

In the night as I gaze at the stars in their flight,
Seeking answers above, seeking all that is right.

Todd joined:

Although nothing is said in response to my plight,
I can see many things that remain out of sight.

145

In the morning, light slowly flooded the world. "Sunday," Todd said, looking out at the mist rising. "Are these jokers even gonna be open?"

"I dunno," Nellie yawned. "This is your plan."

"What *is* the plan?" Toby asked.

"We've almost got it," said Todd. "Jeez, we should've bought an extra set of costumes. No nun in her right mind would sleep in her habit." Todd reviewed the plan for the Bending Sheep. They couldn't use the GPS, but Toby knew the address; they'd find it by trial and error. When they got there, Todd and Nellie would claim that Anthony escaped from their own conversion facility, and they would demand him back.

"Without something from his parents?" Nellie said. "What if this Bates decides to call them?"

"We're hopefully not staying that long," Todd said. "This is just a diversion. We confuse them. Intimidate them. Long enough to get him out of there."

"What if we don't manage to intimidate them?"

"Are you kidding? You as a nun?"

"What if they call the cops?"

"On good Christians like us? We'll drop to our knees and pray. Like good ol' Bump. They won't dare touch us."

"Todd, sweetie, can you credibly drop to your knees and pray?"

"Sure. I mean, how many ways are there to do it?"

"I wouldn't know. I refused to go to church starting at six and a half."

"Six and a half?" Toby said. "What did your parents say?"

"They're pretty liberal. They told people it was a phase and eventually people stopped asking."

"Can we get something to eat?" Toby asked.

"Sure." Todd started the car. "What do nuns eat?"

"I dunno," said Nellie. "Do we want to go into IHOP in these outfits?"

"It'll help us practice!" Todd said. "Then after we abduct Anthony we ditch 'em."

Nellie agreed. Toby was already on his phone, locating an IHOP. "Find it and then turn that thing off!" Nellie ordered. They pulled away from the church and out onto the long, straight two-lane. The rising sun illuminated hawks circling, farm equipment paused in a field, a years-old political sign on a barn.

"Funny thing," Nellie mused as they pulled out.

"What?"

"After I said I wasn't going to church anymore, that night, lying in bed, I guessed I shouldn't pray, since I'd given it all up." They drove through the empty center of a town, the only ones who stopped at the only traffic light. "But it was a tradition. I couldn't just stop. I thought God would miss me, and somehow I couldn't bear that. So I started, like, 'I'm sorry, God, it's nothing personal, I still love You, but I have to do this.' And somehow I kind of fell asleep." They started up again. Just past the center of town, overhead, a big green sign advanced in the sun, pointing the way west. Todd eased onto the exit ramp, and it lifted them into the pink and gold dawn. "And I heard a voice, right in my ear, say, 'If you ever need Me, just call.'"

"That was it?"

All around, the lonely houses shone amidst the corn.

"I sort of forgot, the way six-year-olds do. But now and then I'd remember and think, *Well, maybe someday.*"

"Maybe today," said Toby.

Todd took Nellie's hand. Neither of them wanted to address what would happen after they freed Anthony. Soon came the exit for the IHOP, and they got their first taste of being in public in costume, being addressed as "Sister." Todd smiled demurely while Nellie told the waitress, "Sister doesn't speak. It's a tragic story."

Afterward, full and anxious, they waited by the car while Toby used the men's room.

"So," Todd said, grinning, "first request of God in twelve years is gonna be to whack a gay conversion camp warden?"

Nellie's eyes went wide.

"Kidding!"

"We are not *whacking* anyone!" she said. "We are intimidating someone, lying to someone, and abducting someone. That's very different. No whacking. Where would we even put him?"

"So your strategy is just to pray for a miracle?"

"Why not? But we're gonna do our part. Like you said, we confuse and intimidate 'em, then grab Anthony and run."

"I'd feel better," Todd muttered, "if I had a gun."

"Dude," Nellie said. "You had trouble back there managing your habit while pouring syrup. Look, there's butter on your sleeve. And you think you should be allowed to have a gun?"

"I just think this whole thing might be like on Cracked-dot-com where they have 'Fourteen Plot Holes You Never Noticed in *Star Wars*.' Like, if Leia is—"

"Ix-nay. Toby."

"Speaking of which," Todd went on, "once we have Anthony, what do we—?"

"*Ix-nay*. We'll figure it out."

"Maybe God won't mind you asking Him for a second favor."

"I hope not," Nellie said. She winked at him. "And stop thinking about me and butter!" And they all climbed in the car.

CHAPTER FIFTEEN

A villain defeated, though tragically—A joyous reunion,
which is not without some regret for the past and some fear
for the future—A long-deferred decision at last looms

The Bending Sheep was easily found. The main house with
its wraparound porch and filigree looked perfectly innocent, like a bed-and-breakfast in a movie. It stood at the
top of a long, sloping lawn bound by split-rail fences and
scattered with apple and black walnut trees. Fruit had
begun to fall. The bunkhouses and other facilities were out
of sight.

They eased up the gravel drive. Bay windows framed lace
curtains tied in swags. Wind chimes gently tinkled. In a
meadow beyond the fence a pair of horses flicked away
flies. Where the drive turned around there stood a white
cross. An American flag hung from the porch. A pale,
intense young man in a white shirt, black pants, and black
shoes sat on the porch swing. When the car pulled up, he
rose and stole inside. Todd and Nellie parked and got out.
Toby looked up at the windows, straining to catch sight of
his beloved. He had been told to stay in the car. He would
play the part of another stray they were taking back to their
fold, St. Bonaventure's Home for Effeminate Boys, in a

neighboring state (in a town that did have a St. Bonaventure's church, making their story somewhat credible). On the road, Nellie had practiced addressing Todd as "Sister" and saying "Praise Jesus" every few sentences. Toby had kept cracking up and that cracked Todd and Nellie up, but finally they managed to get through a whole conversation (about buying gas) without losing it. Having warmed up, Nellie then reviewed the case of "poor, misguided Anthony" and "the Satanic impulses that brought him here."

They mounted the porch steps of the Bending Sheep. "So," Todd said. "This is the lair of Satan."

"One smells the stench," Nellie said cheerfully. In fact, they smelled blueberry muffins, one of which Todd hoped aloud that they could have. "Shush!" Nellie said. "You're mute!" In the yard, a little blond boy played by the fence.

"May I help you?"

A man stepped out the front door. He held a meaty paw out to Nellie. "Erasmus Bates," he said, and smiled. "Executive director of the Bending Sheep."

"Sister Evangeline of St. Bonaventure's," Nellie said. Suddenly she began to cough.

"I'm afraid I don't know it," Bates said.

After a few more coughs, Nellie managed to get out, "St. Bonaventure's Home for Effeminate Boys?"

"No," Bates said. "I don't think so." He turned to Todd. "But welcome. It does sound as though we have something in common. And you are?"

Nellie held up a hand. "Sister Richardine doesn't speak," she sighed. Todd took a deep breath. Bates stared. "She, um, was traumatized by a mudslide in the Balkans." Still Bates stared. "We were distributing shovels to the poor," Nellie said brightly. "Near Vilnius. I mean—"

"I think you mean the Bal*tics*," said Bates. He attempted a smile but it got twisted.

"Yes. Those," said Nellie. "Balkans, Baltics, we do so many good works it's difficult to remember."

"At any rate," Bates said, offering Todd a hand, "it's a pleasure to meet you, Sister." They shook. "Goodness me," Bates said. "That's some grip you've got there." Todd watched Bates. Something about that face—

"Sister leads our weightlifting club," Nellie volunteered. "At the convent." When Bates said nothing she added, "In the basement."

"By the way," Bates said, "could I offer either one of you a blueberry muffin?"

Todd nodded vigorously.

Nellie held up her hand. "No," she said. "Sister Richardine and I are fasting until the black sin of homosexuality is eradicated from the face of the Earth."

Todd stared at her bug-eyed.

"We believe," she continued, "that God will come down and, you know, more or less, um, set fire to all the homosexuals—" She checked her watch. "Soon."

"Really?" said Bates.

"At any rate," Nellie said. "Mr. Bates, I am sure you can understand our distress." Todd did his best to look distressed. "One of our little lambs recently decamped from our premises. We thought he would be among our greatest success stories. Oh, dear!" she exclaimed, clasping her hands and looking to Heaven. "How much faith we had in our lovely, sweet, butch little Anthony. He had burned his Lady Gaga CDs, and he vomited at the mere mention of *RuPaul's Drag Race*.

"And then," she continued tearfully, "one dark night, the Devil sent his emissary to our dear Anthony, luring him out of our hallowed home to join a community theater production of, well, we do not speak its name. We call it 'The French Musical.'"

"*Les Misérables*?" Bates said jovially, pronouncing all the s's. "Nothing wrong with that. In fact, we use it as an example here for how a young man should—"

"No no no no no," Nellie said, waving her hand. "The

other one." Bates frowned. In a stage whisper Nellie said, "*La Cage*—?"

"Oh, dear Jesus!" said Bates. He spat on the porch floor. Nellie tried to follow suit, but nerves had dried up her mouth and she could make only a little "Puh!" Then Todd tried, but his loud, extended hocking noise drew a furious stare from Nellie.

To compensate, Todd then fell to his knees, crossed himself, clasped his hands to his breast, and rocked to and fro. Out of the corner of his eye he saw the tow-headed boy in the yard, running with a stick. That jacket . . . Hm.

"Mr. Bates," Nellie wailed. "How we wept into our pillows. Which, as you know, aren't that big. In our cells. Which are very little. As you know." Bates nodded. "And then, Mr. Bates. The news came. We discovered that dear, strapping Anthony was here. Being sort of, uh, re-reeducated. As it were."

Bates frowned. "No, ma'am," he said. "You are mistaken. Anthony's parents placed him here. They said nothing about a 'St. Bonaventure.'"

Todd continued to rock in prayer and to think, *That little boy's jacket . . . His hair . . .*

"Oh!" Nellie sighed. "It pains me to say this, Mr. Bates, but they said nothing because, well, they removed him from us *without paying*. And again, one hates to say it, but anyone who takes him in is thus harboring a fugitive. It certainly wasn't his decision. Anthony loves us! If you might call for him we could clear up everything—"

That little blond head . . .

Bates held up a hand. "Wait wait wait!" he said. "Hold everything." Nellie tried to speak but he held up his hand again. "This whole thing smells fishy. I've never heard of this St. Bonaventure, and frankly, the two of you don't look much like nuns or like anyone in any position of authority!"

Todd stood. Nellie and Bates looked at him. He took a step toward Bates. He heard Nellie's intake of breath. "Let me tell you about my position of authority, Mr. Bates," Todd said.

"Ha! I knew it!" Bates exulted. "You two—"

"That's your son over there, isn't it?" Todd demanded.

"Hey, buddy, you stay away from my boy. I'll call the cops on both of you right now!"

"And he was with you," Todd continued, "in your car a few days ago when you parked at the rest stop off Interstate 69 between South Hook and Fort Troy."

Bates was stunned. He glanced at his son, then back at Todd.

"When you were *cruising me*," Todd said coolly.

"I don't know what you're talking about." Bates nearly choked on the words.

"You think I don't remember?" Todd sneered. Nellie had her phone out. She held Bates's emails up to him. "You're the one," Todd pronounced, "who begged. Could your *kid* come along? Your poor, innocent son! We have every email! I wonder, Mr. Bates, how many *other* guys from around here could ID you?" Bates's face was white. "If I posted an ad: 'Calling all guys who've had sex with the Dad of the Year who brought his little blond son along.' Who'd recognize you? Who's out there at some liberal rag, rubbing their hands over the prospect of a story like this? I can see it now: 'George Takei Destroys Reverend Bates in One Perfect Tweet.' 'J. K. Rowling Trolls Reverend Bates in One Perfect Tweet.'"

"'Pope Francis,'" Nellie said, "Destroys Rev—"

Bates scoffed, but his breathing was labored and he was sweating. "No one would believe it," he sneered. "I'm a pillar of my community!"

"You're a pillar of the men's room on I-69," Todd sneered, "to which you bring a child. Who waits while Daddy and his 'pillar'—"

"Dear God, you shut up!" Bates put a finger in Todd's face. With his other hand, he fumbled with his own cell. "I am calling the cops—*now!*"

"Well, then," Todd said, "we had better go, hadn't we?"

"That's what I would strongly suggest," Bates growled.

"But you'll never know what we might tell," Todd said. "Or to whom we tell it. So I would suggest, Mr. Bates, that you negotiate with us now. While you have the chance."

The hand with the cell phone tensed. "I do not negotiate," Bates snarled. He turned on Nellie. "What are you doing?" he demanded.

Nellie had Ferdslist open on her phone. "What was it you said? 'Calling all guys who'—?"

Bates lunged at her. "Give me that!"

Todd aimed his own phone and hit the video icon. "Here it is, folks," he announced. "Mr. Pillar beating up a nun!"

Nellie screamed and fell down. "He's raping me!" she yelled. The little boy stopped in his tracks and watched.

"Now," Todd said, coming around to get the boy in the frame, "here we see Pillar's poor little boy, watching."

Bates went for Todd. "You leave my son out of this!" he thundered.

"Why?" Todd sneered. "You don't!'"

"Just get Anthony!" Nellie snapped, jumping to her feet. "And this will be over."

A police cruiser swung in through the main gate. Before Todd or Nellie could think, Bates ran to its open window. "Shit!" Nellie said. "What do we do?"

"I'm having them arrest you for naming me 'Sister Richardine,'" said Todd.

"Please!" Nellie snapped. "It could have been way worse. When I was a kid, there was a Sister Insemenata."

"And a mudslide in the Balkans?"

"Fine! I'm sorry! Next time we script *everything* in advance."

"And you owe me a muffin."

They could not hear what Bates said to the cops, but they saw him holding his hands out, as though pushing down on something. His tone was chatty, though they could not make out the words. The cop behind the wheel grinned. Then they were on their way.

Bates swaggered back, jaw set. He came up to Todd and Nellie, eyes blazing. "You two consider yourselves lucky!" he snarled. "I'm in the right, and I know it. You are some kind of criminals. But. The number one thing my board wants is no controversy. And I have to bow to them."

"And I bet you do it well," Todd said.

"Listen, buddy, I could have you in jail in two seconds. I would prevail. No one would believe you. You are ridiculous. But my board wouldn't like the allegation. The world is full of people wanting to tell lies about the consecrated work I do. I have to field vicious allegations like yours weekly!"

"Daddy?" The little boy stumbled toward Bates, a stick in his hand.

"Later, son, okay?" Bates said.

"Daddy, can we go to the rest stop?"

Bates shuddered suddenly but still spoke calmly and tenderly. "I said 'later'!"

"Daddy, *please!*" The boy turned to Todd and announced. "When we go to the rest stop, I get Oreos!"

Todd felt ill. Bates's pale face quivered.

"Plus, sometimes," the boy went on, "I get to watch a movie on my tablet!" He counted on his fingers. "I watched *Moana* and *Kung-Fu Panda* and *Despicable Me*, and—"

"That's enough, son," Bates whimpered. "Please, just go and play."

"If I go play, can we go to the rest stop later?"

Bates closed his eyes. Todd prepared to catch him if he fell. Then his eyes opened. Todd thought, *This is the saddest face I have ever seen.* "Yes," Bates said, almost inaudibly. "We can."

The boy trotted off. "Yippee!" he cried. "We're going to the rest stop!"

Bates winced. Suddenly the boy turned back. "I love you, Daddy!" he screamed, and dashed off.

Bates turned listlessly toward the house, barely able to raise his arm to beckon. When he did, the door opened. The young man in the white shirt and black pants bustled out over the lawn, kicking up dew. His hair was a helmet, flecked with dandruff, his mouth a twitching line, his arms thin and veiny, his nails too long. He eyed Nellie and Todd, and his lip twitched.

"Oliver," Bates sighed. "Bring Anthony out, please." His eyelids drooped. His body swayed.

"Anthony?" Oliver demanded.

"Yes, Oliver." Bates's voice was just a whisper. "Bring Anthony out. Now, please."

In the meadow the boy's voice exulted, "Going to the rest stop! Going to the rest stop!" Bates's jaw twitched. Oliver did not move. Bates did not look at him, just stood and swayed. Finally, with a sniff, Oliver turned on his heel and bustled back to the house. They could hear his toes kicking the grass. The door creaked open, then slammed. Seconds passed.

"You will never, ever, ever," Bates managed to croak out, "speak a word of what you *claim* to know." He shot Todd a look. "Never."

"Never," Todd said quietly.

"I admit nothing. I have broken no laws. I am turning this young man over to you because he was on the verge of being expelled anyway. And as I said, my board wants no trouble. They would never question my integrity."

The front door creaked. Anthony, thin and stooped, stumbled onto the porch, pushed by Oliver, who kept a grip on his arm. Down the steps he shoved him, then pulled him along, stumbling, across the grass. When at last they reached Bates, Todd, and Nellie, Oliver shoved Anthony away and stood at attention, hands clasped behind his back.

"That will be all, Oliver," Bates sighed. "Thank you."

Oliver shook his head and rolled his eyes.

"Oliver," Bates announced, looking Anthony up and down, "is one of our *success* stories! Wanted to be a *fashion designer!* Playing with whatever you call them. *Swatches.*" He drew close to Anthony, who kept his head down. "Mincing up and down! Sighing and whining." Closer still. "And do you know what he is now? Quarterback of our football team! Had his first girl on his furlough a couple of weeks ago."

"That's where I know that face from!" Nellie said. Bates scowled at her. "That chick in Wyler City accused him of rape. I saw it online."

Bates's eyes blazed. "Listen, Missy," he snarled, "no one gets it just right the first time. And it's a biological fact that women like masculine men. They like being forced. They like having men take over. That's what Oliver learned, and he learned it well. And no charges have been filed. You keep that in mind, 'Sister.' Whatever you are. You look like you know a thing or two about men taking you over! Now, you got your little pansy. Get him outta here and get yourselves outta here before I change my mind and bring that cop back."

Anthony looked fearfully at Todd and then at Nellie. "Wh-who are you?" he asked tremulously. "Do I know you?"

Nellie reached a hand out to him. "We come from St. *Tobias's* Church," she said. Anthony let her take his arm.

"You remember *St. Tobias's*, don't you?" Todd said. "We're going to take you *back there*." He glanced at Bates, who kept silent.

"Um, okay," said Anthony.

"Where you'll be safe," Nellie promised.

"You remember *St. Tobias's* motto, don't you?" Todd said. "How all love is legitimate?"

Suddenly Anthony smiled. A tear came to his eye. "Sure," he said. His smiled broadened, and he pointed at Todd. "You're from Fleet High, right?"

"I minister to them occasionally," Todd said. The three fell in step together, moving toward the car.

"Now," Nellie said, "we are going to get in and drive away with as little fanfare as possible. Public displays of affection will be saved for once we're on the interstate."

"Public displays?" Anthony asked.

"Yes," Nellie said. "As soon as we're out of sight of that lunatic. Are you all right, by the way? Do you need a doctor or anything?"

Anthony cringed a little. "I think maybe so," he said. "But what public displays—?"

Nellie opened the car door to reveal Toby crouched down.

"Oh, my God!" Anthony gasped.

"Easy, easy," Todd said. "Der Führer is watching, and we are on very thin ice—Toby, down!—Anthony, just get in—"

Which Anthony did, and immediately Toby wrapped himself around his lover.

"Now, you said 'maybe so' to a doctor?" Nellie asked.

"Well . . ." Anthony looked at each of them. His eyes filled with tears.

"What, sweetie?" said Toby.

"I was sort of thinking I wish a doctor could look at—I can't say it."

In a cold voice Todd demanded, "What did he do? What did that—?"

"Nothing," said Anthony. "Nothing that doesn't happen to a lot of guys here. If you fail—"

"You have not failed at anything!" said Nellie. She got behind the wheel. Toby hugged Anthony tighter.

"Did he rape you?" Todd growled.

"Maybe . . ." Anthony whimpered.

Todd froze.

To Toby, Anthony cried softly, "I'm sorry!" Toby held him close and just repeated, "Shh! It's all right!"

Todd started across the lawn.

"No!" Nellie said. She ran after him, wimple flapping, shouting, "We don't have time!"

Todd wheeled around. "There is always time to do what is right," he said. Behind Nellie came Anthony. "Ask them about a guy named Joshua!" he called. Todd turned again toward the house and his legs got tangled in his habit. "Jesus Christ!" he growled. He pulled the whole costume off, threw it down, and proceeded to march up to the house in his T-shirt and tighty-whities. "Try to get Joshua, too!" Anthony called, bent over and panting. Nellie ran to him and held him. "Joshua! Please!"

Todd opened the door. There stood Oliver, who babbled, "Hey! Um, you . . . excuse me . . . ?" His gaze went up and down Todd's legs and around his chest and torso.

"Where is he?" Todd demanded.

"Who? Wait, you can't—"

Todd came at Oliver and Oliver quickly pointed.

A moment later Todd plowed into Bates's office.

Bates stared, speechless, his gaze tracing the same path over Todd's body that Oliver's had.

"Yeah," Todd said. "Here it is. What you wanted. Take a good look, 'cause you're not seeing it for long."

"You're keeping your promise, aren't you?" Bates snapped, staring at Todd's chest and then at his crotch.

"No," Todd said. "You *raped* him. Him and a hundred others. A thousand. No. You're going down, buddy."

Bates's face collapsed, his lip quivered, and tears leaked from his eyes. Still he stole glances at Todd's body.

"Sure!" Todd said. "Where were the tears when those boys were alone in their cells, bleeding? You are evil incarnate, Bates, and we are telling the world!"

Bates's mouth opened and closed silently as he wept. Finally he managed to say, "I'm . . . sorry . . . I-I'm . . . sor . . . ry . . ." He came around his desk, reaching for Todd, who backed away. Bates fell to his knees repeating, "I'm sorry!" and looked up at Todd's strapping form. "All I wanted," he wept, "all I wanted . . . His name was . . . Ben. He came to our school in fourth grade. He was the most beautiful boy ever. I didn't know there could be a boy like that. It was like I'd been waiting for him. I prayed to God to make him my friend. I tried to do everything he'd like. I joined clubs he was in. At Christmas I asked my parents for a shirt like one Ben had. But when I wore it he took one look at me and said, 'Oh, gross!' But I couldn't stop . . . loving him. And loving . . . other boys. I prayed, but every time I spoke to Him, God said, 'Oh, gross!' And then at church . . . they told me they could do something. To change me. To make God like me again." For a few seconds Bates just wept. Then he continued. "But He never did. I tried everything. Got married, had a son . . ." He got up and went to the window. "I named him . . . Ben! God never liked me. But at least he stopped saying, 'Oh, gross.' Like I said, I am a pillar." He looked up at Todd beseechingly. "You can't! Please! I promise I'll stop. I just don't know how. The directors want results!"

Todd folded his arms and shook his head. "I can't take the chance," he said. "You're a rapist."

"No!" Bates wailed, falling again to the carpet and curling up like a fetus.

"I will, though, give you seventy-two hours to turn yourself in."

Bates just sobbed. Out the window Todd saw Nellie pacing. "Starting now," Todd said. "That's it." He turned and exited the office. As he went for the front door, Oliver materialized from the shadows. "Hey!" Oliver hissed. "Hey, can we meet later? This is my number!" Todd pushed him aside, then abruptly stopped and turned. He ignored the scrap of paper with the phone number. "You got a kid here named Joshua?" Todd demanded. Confusion played over Oliver's face. "He ran away," he stammered. Todd seized him. "I swear!" Oliver squeaked. "Vanished! Gone! Two days ago! We reported it!" Todd shoved him away and charged out across the lawn.

Watching Todd come toward the car in T-shirt and underpants, Nellie said, "Damn!"

Toby just smiled and said, "Hm." He had seen Todd in less.

And then a gunshot rang out. They heard Oliver's scream, and they saw the little boy trot toward the house, then slow down and call, "Daddy! What was that noise?"

Todd dove into the car and Nellie floored it. "Put the costume back on," she said. Turning in his seat Todd told Anthony, "No Joshua. He ran away." Then he asked Nellie, "Why? You said that after we did this we could—"

"That's good," Anthony said. "I guess."

"Because Bates is not the issue," Nellie said. "He won't talk now. The cops back home are the issue."

Toby asked who Joshua was.

"And they," Nellie concluded, "aren't looking for nuns."

"Someone I wronged," Anthony said, staring out the window. But he would say no more.

"They were *terrible!*" Toby rolled his eyes as he snuggled Anthony in the back seat and the car sped west. "'A mud-slide in the Balkans.' 'Sister Richardine.'"

"I will have you know," Nellie said severely, "that is a culturally accurate nun name."

"Yeah," said Toby, "but Vilnius is not culturally or accurately in the Balkans. And *then*," he said, "the thing about *small pillows!*"

"Small *what?*" said Anthony.

"Excuse me," said Todd, "are we maybe sort of getting to the part where someone says, 'Thanks to you, our elders and betters, we are now freed from the vise-grip of hetero-normative oppression'?"

"Not even close," said Toby. "Basically, this whole thing succeeded because I crouched down so brilliantly." Anthony kissed him all over his face and Toby kissed back.

"Would someone at least," Todd asked, "find me another Party Hearty so I can get a culturally accurate priest costume?"

"No!" Nellie said. "In fact, all cell phones off. Right now." She called into the back seat. "You two included. Off, off."

"Why?" Anthony demanded.

"Because," Nellie explained as she swung up onto the interstate, "they may be following us."

"Who?" Anthony asked.

"The authorities, let's just say," Nellie sighed.

"For posing as nuns?"

"That's the least of our problems. Like I said, it could even help." Nellie noticed that Toby had gone quiet. "We're kind of fleeing from sort of a misunderstanding that might now include kidnapping of a minor." She paused and then whimpered, "Oh, God, my parents!" She turned to Todd and said softly, "We should head for the coast."

"Right-o," Todd sighed. The thought of his own mother, alone and confused, was almost too much to bear. "And whatever you do," he added, "don't speed!"

"Seventy is my middle name," Nellie said.

"And we have to go with you?" Anthony inquired.

"For now," Nellie said. There was a long silence. "Just for now." And then there was only the hum of the tires.

Finally Todd asked, "What about my costume? And my muffin?"

"Anthony can find a Party Hearty on his phone. The cops don't know about him. But once we find it, that's it. No phones, and we pay cash for everything. Fortunately, we have a fair amount. And if there's a Dunkin', we'll get you a muffin."

"Where do we stay?" Todd asked.

"Days Inn takes cash," said Nellie.

"But then the car sits in a parking lot. Right where—"

"Worse than that." Nellie blew out a breath and hunkered down in the driver's seat. "They ask for your license plate, at the desk. And we'd run out of money in a week."

"What about Walmart?" Toby interjected.

"What *about* Walmart?" said Todd.

"People camp in Walmart parking lots," Toby said.

"And the cops let them?"

"Walmart lets them," Toby said. "It's private property. I guess the people who do it shop at the Walmart and so they allow it."

Anthony stuck his phone over into the front seat. "There's a Party Hearty in another four exits," he said.

"Get me the name and number," Nellie said, "then turn the phone off and keep it off."

Four exits later they swerved into a Party Hearty parking lot and got Todd a priest costume, then headed back to the highway. The sun was all the way up and the Bending Sheep seemed far behind them.

"Walmart, ho!" said Todd.

No one else said anything, though later Toby could be heard whispering, "It's all right, it's all right" to his lover, who quietly whimpered, "No, it isn't. No, it isn't."

CHAPTER SIXTEEN

Sister Bonaventure in the wilderness—An account of suffering and loss, such as befalls our fellow citizens all too often in these troubled times—The forgotten emerge from the shadows, daring to believe grace may be theirs— Our friends' journey intersects the journey of another

Fields flew by under bright sun. Sex shops looked like bunkers lit up with neon. They pulled up to a liquor store to ask where a Walmart was. "Our order doesn't believe in technology," Nellie stammered, when the manager suggested she look on her phone. The guy took out his own phone and searched. She went back to the car with scribbled directions. "There's one close, but not in the best area. There was a fight two weeks ago. He had all this advice. Don't play loud music or litter. Don't park near the doors—like, near the real shoppers? And it's considered good form to buy something."

They continued west as the sun fell. Toby reached into the front seat and put his arm around Todd. Todd held his hand, and Anthony his other hand.

"Well," Todd said. "At least no one's gonna start a brawl with a nun." He caressed Nellie's face.

"Title of my autobiography," Nellie murmured wistfully.

"Are we going to Walmart, too?" Anthony asked. "I mean, I'm super grateful and everything, but, how much longer—?"

"Not much," Todd said. "I promise."

There was an awkward silence.

"We know," Toby said. He patted Todd's chest. "You don't wanna say goodbye to us 'cause we're so cute!"

A moment later everyone saw—but no one commented—that Todd had begun to cry. Then Nellie. And finally the boys.

Purple clouds moved over the vast, bright lot. The last orange-pink smudge faded in the west. On someone's radio a country station went in and out. Kids ran barefoot with a dog with a bandanna around its neck and a length of electrical cord for a leash. An old man limped to his car with a sagging plastic bag. "Need to wash that car!" he called to them, and grinned. He was missing some teeth. "Oh! Sorry, Sister!"

"Jesus!" Nellie said. "The nun thing!"

"We gotta," said Todd. "It might save our butts."

Nellie put her nose to her shoulder as she steered. "This thing is getting rank. Can I get a sponge bath in the rest room?"

"Maybe that guy would let you shower in his RV!" said Todd.

"I just might." She steered the car to a space far from the store and not near any other vehicles.

"Can we get food?" Anthony asked.

"Please do!" Todd handed him some bills. Anthony hesitated. "Go on," said Todd. "I assume they discharged you penniless."

Anthony hung his head and took the money. Toby opened the door.

When they were gone, Todd told Nellie, "I was gonna

remind them not to hold hands in there, but it sounded too, well, you know. Maybe I should go with them."

Nellie smiled and said, "Gotta let your kids go someday."

Todd hugged himself. Nellie had an impulse to put her arms around him, but she was pretty sure nuns did not touch priests. That way, at least. "Let's get some air," she said.

No sooner had Nellie swung open the door than a plump, red-faced man with stubble and a baseball cap ("Random's Feed and Grain, Wyler City") waved to her and called, "Sister!"

"My son," Nellie managed to say. The man came to her. His fleshy, unshaven face drooped. Todd came around the car to the two of them.

"Sister, I hope I'm not intruding," the man said and stopped to catch his breath. "But I am so happy to see you. I'm parked over there. I been here four nights. So much has gone wrong. I'm supposed to be taking these pills. Maybe you've heard of them. Paxil? Anyway, and my dog's sick, and I don't have enough for the pills *and* to take Sparkplug to the vet—that's my dog—but, gosh darn it, if he— He's all I have in the world, Sister. He's my only friend. This morning I got on my knees for the first time in twelve, thirteen years. Got down and prayed to God for a sign. Now, here you are. Here you *both* are! Ministering to the poor and forgotten. That's who's here, mostly. Folks with no place else to go. Sister, would you, or, no, maybe the Father would hear my confession?"

"Sure!" said Todd.

"We are something of a liberal order," Nellie interrupted. "I can hear it, too."

"Really?" the man said. "Well, all right. Like I said, it's been a long time, but this morning when Sparkplug coughed so bad, I thought God must be mad at me and that's why he made Sparkplug so sick, so maybe if I confessed— And now, like I say, here you are!" The man

167

himself coughed again. He took Todd's hand in both of his. "Thank you, Father!" he said. "And thank you, Sister. My name's Herb, by the way. Should we, um, well, where should we do this? I mean, is now a good time, or—?"

"Good a time as any!" Todd said. "Why don't we just step around the other side of the car and have some privacy?" Night had fallen, and bright lights were on overhead. They made their way to a strip of grass away from the cars. Todd went on: "So, Herb," he said, "as, um, Sister Bonaventure said, our order is a bit, you know, liberal."

Herb nodded.

"So we don't have a lot of formalities," Todd said. "You just have to"—he searched his memory for movie or TV scenes with confessions—"to say, um, 'Bless me, Father. And Sister—'"

". . . for I have sinned," Herb concluded.

"Right! And then, um—"

"It's been thirteen years since my last confession."

"Yes. And then, you know, away you go!"

"Okay," Herb said. He removed his cap and patted his bald head. "I've been pretty bad, I guess. Let's see. I used to drink a lot. That's where it began. I don't no more. Maybe a beer now and then. I didn't go to AA or nothin'." He replaced the cap. "Where I was, it was too far, and my wife and me couldn't afford more'n one car. This other fella was going to drive me, but he was in a accident and couldn't. There's phone meetings, too, but they cut off my phone. I couldn't pay, and that was because of the drinking. So I said, 'Gosh darn, I'm going to do it myself. I'm gonna make myself stop!' And I pretty nearly have. Just a beer now and then, like I said.

"Then my wife went to find work in another state. Her and my daughter. We agreed it was best. I guess I knew, then. I knew, you know, she wasn't coming back. We'd talk on the phone. She paid for my phone to be, like, reactivated. But then we weren't talking so much. I tried to talk to my little girl once a week. But if I said, 'Put Mommy on,' my wife'd be busy. We were high school sweethearts. I thought we'd always be together. I just thought, I mean, that's what we said when we got married. I remember that day. It was sunny and— And now, all I got is Sparkplug. I want to ask my wife, 'Where did we go wrong?' You remember how happy everyone was, and then the bills come. Anyway, I got another job. I thought that might change her mind. Even went to a couple of those meetings. Bought a van. A used one. But they weren't coming back. And, well, I don't know if it's a sin, but I had these moods. That's what the Paxil's for, but, you see, that job ended, the one that paid for the Paxil. The insurance paid for the Paxil, and that job ended.

"But I'd made a promise to Sparkplug that he'd never go hungry, plus my little girl, I sent her money, too. Well, I sent it to my wife, even though she wasn't speaking to me. Sometimes I went without the Paxil, and with having the moods it was tough to get a job. And now Sparkplug's so sick, Sister. And it's all because I was bad! Just bad bad bad!"

Herb started to cry. Nellie blinked away her own tears and assured Herb, "Our order doesn't believe that anyone's 'bad.'"

"What about original sin?" Herb said, alarmed.

"Well, yes," Nellie said. "That applies to everyone."

"But we don't judge," Todd said. "We don't believe God punishes."

"Really?" said Herb.

"God looks on you and Sparkplug with compassion," said Nellie. Out of the corner of her eye she noticed the boys were standing a way off.

"You know the worst thing?" Herb said. "The worst thing I thought?"

"What?" Nellie asked.

"Sometimes, at, you know, three or four a.m., parked out

here, when Sparkplug wakes up coughing, I think, gosh, if he dies, then maybe I'll be able to afford to get back on my feet! And when I think that, I just, I bang my head on the steering wheel, or punch myself like this." Herb swung a fist at his temple without making contact. "I think, if I do that, I can make the thoughts just go away."

"Herb," Nellie said, laying her hand on his shoulder, "when you hit your head like that, it hurts God. Even more than it hurts you. You must treat all of God's creations tenderly, yourself included." She glanced at the boys. They held bags of food and watched.

"But then, what'll I do, Sister, without—? He's all I have. Maybe I don't deserve to have anything. Maybe God's just forgotten about me."

"No," Todd said. "God never forgets."

"I got a theory," Herb said. "Maybe it's a sin to say it, but I got a theory God's up there working hard to make good, perfect, worthwhile people. The best people He can. Only it's hard. So He's got a lot of discards." He pointed to the store. "Like, in there, they got 'irregular' underwear they sell for a discount. God's got irregular discards, like me, and He tosses us down here and we make our way around while the good people, the people who've done things right, the ones He made the right way, they get the money and nice homes and get married and go to universities. Is that a sin, Sister, to think that?"

"I would have to say," Nellie admitted, "that our order disapproves of the idea that you are a 'discard.' Thinking that is, in fact, a sin. But an understandable one. And of course we forgive you."

"Of course," Todd echoed. "And God forgives you."

"Especially God," Nellie agreed. "And Jesus."

"So, um, do I have to do anything more?" Herb asked. "I mean, I guess that's my confession. Is there, you know, penance?"

"You could recite some Hail Marys," Todd suggested. "I

mean, you don't have to—" He tried to remember what, in fact, a Hail Mary was.

"I'd say, go be with Sparkplug," Nellie said. "He needs you."

Herb nodded and wiped a tear away. "I will. Thank you, Sister. Thank you, Father. I'll go be with him now." Herb again looked at them as though unsure what to do. He seemed to want to shake hands or say more, but in the end he hurried off toward his trailer, waving and calling, "Thank you" as he went.

Nellie looked at Todd. Both exhaled and slumped. The boys came forward with muffins and iced coffee. Then Nellie and Todd saw what they had not before:

Dozens more people had gathered, waiting a respectful distance away. As Todd and Nellie wolfed muffins and gulped coffee, more people approached and asked them to hear their confessions, or just to talk to them. Some were on crutches or in wheelchairs and asked to be healed. Some had sick children. Some had children who had run away or were in prison. Some hadn't worked in months. The two of them found the stories overwhelming, but soon the advice and prayers became easier to give. ("Stick close to me," Todd had whispered to Nellie. "We have to agree on doctrine.")

Things hit a snag when a portly, exhausted-looking woman in her seventies waddled up to Todd and said, in the saddest, most sincere voice, "Father, please, please pray that my nephew will be cured of the evil disease of homosexuality!"

Todd took the woman's hand. "And is that your nephew's wish?" he asked. The woman hesitated. "Or is it yours?"

"It's God's wish!" the woman said.

"In our order," Todd began, "we avoid praying for the soul to be changed."

"Because the soul comes from God," Nellie said.

"The soul is the breath of God," Todd said, simultaneously thinking, *Good one, Sweeney!* And then, *Jeez, I hope it was sort of right!*

"But we can pray for your nephew's happiness," said Nellie.

"And that he has the strength to do the will of God," Todd added, "whatever that will may be."

The woman looked confused and irritated. "I just know he's sick and going to Hell," she said. "And I want you to stop it!"

Todd nodded. He kept the woman's hand in his, and he looked up. "How often," he said to the crowd, "do we want God to 'just stop' something for us? To 'just do' something for us? We're so sure something is 'bad' or 'wrong.' We know it causes pain. We want it to stop. But do we know that that thing is against the will of God?"

The woman pulled her hand away and, muttering to herself, vanished into the crowd. Others came forward. Some were hungry, so the boys split up the muffins and started handing out pieces. Amazingly, there was enough for everybody. Some of the overhead lights began to go out. Nellie and Todd went through the entire crowd. Word had spread, and some came from the farthest corners of the lot, even from inside the store. Some came from nearby houses. One family with a sick son and another son out of work had driven over an hour to be there. "I sure as hell hope we're not on the news," Nellie muttered to Todd. Anthony overheard. "Not so far," he said, scrolling on his phone. "We're monitoring."

"Well, don't!" Nellie hissed. "No phones!"

"Oops, sorry!" Anthony switched off the phone. "Hey, you've got one more penitent there."

Nellie turned to look. A small-boned, smooth-faced, defiant-looking young man stood there in a T-shirt, jeans, and sneakers. Though he had to be at least Toby's and Anthony's age he had the look of a smart, tough third grader. "Yes, my child?" Nellie said.

"'My child'?" said Toby. "We're not in *The Sound of Music*."

"Tobias," Nellie said pleasantly. "Can we please remember the Golden Rule? Um, rather, can we remember that silence is golden? Which is a rule. Of mine. Yes, young man?"

The young man took a step closer, his jaw thrust out. Nellie looked him up and down and decided that perhaps he had not always been a young man. "What is your name?" she asked.

"Jac," he said. "With a 'c.' No 'k.'"

"Well, Jac-with-a-c-no-k," said Nellie, "what can I do for you?"

Jac shrugged. "Dunno."

"Everyone has a story to tell," Todd said.

He shrugged again.

"When did you start your transition?" Anthony asked from where he and Toby sat on the hood. Jac went to them. "Last year," he said. He confirmed that "he" was indeed his pronoun.

Jac would not say exactly what help he wanted. He said he just came over because he'd heard "the Sister doesn't judge." He explained, "So I just wanted to be near you. Y'know, you can never relax. You think you're being you, but you're a minute away from being bashed or insulted. That's why I left home. My mother threatened to kill me. She said I already killed her daughter, so it'd be fair."

"How long have you been here?" Todd asked.

"A month," Jac said. "That's my tent over there. The Walmart people let me sweep up sometimes. Well, one lady does. She's nice. She pays me cash. I guess it's really just her taking care of me. She tells me the others can't see me. But she says it can't go on forever. Her husband's got em-emphysema? He needs drugs she can't afford. Plus, wherever they go, she has to go there first and count the steps from wherever to wherever. See if there's resting places. If she stops paying me, I gotta move on. And, like, I know this is crazy, but I sometimes think, wouldn't it be nice if someone like her could, like, ride the train ahead of me and tell me what'll happen to me, just like she goes and figures out how her husband's gonna walk places. But no one can do that. I've ridden the rails. You hang around. You get to know people. It's not hard. So long as you stay alert. Guy tried something with me. Near Albuquerque. Said he'd never had a 'tranny.' Said he has friends who'd wanna try, too. I showed him my knife and said he could try it up his ass. I threw him off the train. I guess that was a sin."

"That doesn't mean God doesn't understand," Todd said.

"It was self-defense," said Nellie.

The moon was high and the partiers had quieted. Jac said he had to go. "When you people leaving?" he asked.

"Sunrise," Nellie said.

Jac nodded. "Safe travels," he said.

"You, too," Nellie said, as he turned away.

They were approached a few more times. At last, though, they were able to eat and bed down in the car.

As they were getting in, Anthony, who had seemed about to say something, spoke up. "Um, I have a little confession?" He looked at Nellie. "If you could—?"

"What is it, sweetie?" said Toby.

"We'll talk," Anthony promised. He smiled. "It's just, she's got the uniform and everything!"

Nellie led Anthony to the edge of the lot, close by two older guys reminiscing over tea. A cat mewed. There Anthony told Nellie the story of the terrible decision he had been forced to make about Joshua. Nellie assured him that Bates had offered him "the Devil's choice," and there was no way to win. "Joshua understands, I'm sure," she said. But she wondered if there was any such thing as understanding or forgiveness left in a boy who had been so abused, just because of the pure soul he had been born with.

"What'll happen to those guys at the Sheep?" Anthony wondered. "Their parents will put them someplace else. It's hard to find a friend out here. There's the Internet. But you drive twenty or fifty miles, the guy is drunk, his wife comes home. Or he's got those oxygen things up his noise. But he's nice. Drive another fifty home. Radio says you're a sinner. In the morning the sun just shines on the stone buildings, forever."

When they came back to the car, Todd and Toby were asleep, holding hands between front seat and back. Nellie slipped in next to Todd. Anthony nestled against Toby and held his other hand. Outside the lot had quieted. A few cars passed. Soon all four of them had passed into sleep—a sleep shattered at four in the morning by a pounding on the window, right by Nellie's ear.

"Hey!" a voiced yelled. "Hey! Wake up!"

CHAPTER SEVENTEEN

A dear friend's final hour—
A simple and touching ceremony—Westward, ho!—
The final moment comes—An angel of mercy appears

Nellie and Todd jerked awake, hearts pounding. Nellie put on her sympathetic-but-determined face and rolled the window down. It was Herb.

"Please, Sister," he wept. "I think Sparkplug is going, right now. Sister, is it a sin for you to give last rites to a dog?"

Dazed, Nellie said the first thing that came to mind: "Stop talking about sins!"

The boys were awake now, too, shivering. Everyone piled out of the car and followed Herb. "Do you know the last rites?" Nellie whispered to Todd, who didn't.

Sparkplug, a black Lab gone gray around the muzzle, was huddled, eyes closed, breath shallow and irregular, in a nest of towels in the back of Herb's van. His eyes were cloudy. Every now and then he let out a little wail.

"Oh, Sparkplug!" Herb said, taking the dog's head in his hands. "I guess now's the time, huh, fella?" He put his face down so their noses touched. Sparkplug's tail gave a slow wag. "I'm gonna miss ya, buddy. But I guess you'll be outta pain, so that'll be good. You've been a loyal friend, Sparkplug. I'll never forget you. Um, Sister? Father?"

Since no one knew how to conduct last rites, Todd told Herb that their order didn't exactly approve of last rites for animals, but that they could certainly bless Sparkplug.

"I guess doggies don't go to Heaven," Herb said, "so this is it."

This was more than Nellie could bear. Though Todd had declined to give last rites, she did allow that Herb would see Sparkplug again. She took one of Sparkplug's paws in her hands. Todd took another paw and prayed that Sparkplug would be out of pain and that he would know how much Herb loved him. Through tears Nellie said, "It's time for you to run free, Sparkplug."

"Run to God, Sparkplug!" Herb said, gasping, tears running down his face.

A few minutes later, with a hollow wheeze and a last whimper, Sparkplug went. Herb held him in his arms and rocked his lifeless body and cried till he could cry no more. Then he asked, "What now? Guess we bury him somewhere, huh?"

"Yes, indeed," Todd said. He could not help but worry how this interfered with their plans for escaping. But, just as he had wondered at the rest area what Race would do, now he wondered how the priest that he was not would react. More charitably, he thought.

"You know," Nellie said, sniffling, "back home—I mean, at the nunnery. The convent. We watch a lot of British mysteries and things. I mean, after we pray. And do good works and things. And I have noticed," she continued gamely, "that whenever things look bad for the British, they make tea. Now, Herb, I see a hot pot there, and some Lipton's, so why don't we all have a cup of tea and take a deep breath and plan a little celebration of Sparkplug's life."

Herb nodded. Gently he lay Sparkplug down, looked at him a moment, and then folded the towels over him and sobbed and sobbed.

Water roared in the hot pot.

"Herb," Todd asked gently, "do you have a shovel?"

"Yes, sir!" Herb said. "I do."

"Next door to here," Todd said, "there's an empty field, and we could bury him there. Before it gets too light."

Nellie placed tea bags and poured water in five Styrofoam cups of suspect cleanliness. Everyone drank anyway, then got to work.

Herb carried Sparkplug, wrapped in towels. Anthony brought a black garbage bag and Todd the shovel. They walked out across the parking lot to the field and dug. A gray-orange glow appeared around the horizon.

Herb wrote a note to Sparkplug that he wouldn't let anyone see and tucked it inside the towels. Then he put Sparkplug in the garbage bag. To the bag he attached another note. He begged anyone who dug up the field and found the bag to rebury Sparkplug in a fitting place. He wrote out his email address, so they could tell him. Everyone took turns digging the hole deeper as the sky grew lighter. At six-thirty Todd pronounced it deep enough.

"This is it, buddy," Herb said, cradling the bag. "I'm sorry I have to leave you here, but you know times are hard. You were a good dog, Sparkplug. You were the best. I couldn't have survived and met these fine people, if it hadn't been for you."

Todd asked to see Herb's phone. Online he found text to say over the grave. Everyone knew the necessity of hitting the road, but they let Herb tell the story of how Sparkplug was so loyal and lifted his spirits so many times when things were bad. Suddenly the sun flooded the fields. Herb said he guessed they had best wrap up. He couldn't bring himself to watch as Toby shoveled dirt over the black

179

parcel that suddenly seemed so small. He went and stood by himself till it was over.

Then everyone hugged awkwardly and left the gravesite quickly. Herb went to his van. "I'll find me another lot somewhere," he said. He began to cry again. "But not another dog. Not ever." The friends all consoled him, then hugged him again and went for their car. As they got to it, Todd said, "Wait a second." He ran to the edge of the lot, to a small pop-up tent on a patch of grass. "Hey!" he said. "Hey!" He shook the tent.

"Who is it?" Jac's face appeared, sleepy. "I got a knife!"

"Cool it with the hardware!" Todd said. "You got five minutes to pack and come with us."

"Say what?"

"Five minutes!" And he ran back toward his car.

When he got there, Nellie said, "You didn't."

"Of course I did," said Todd. "What else was I going to do?"

"Well, yeah," Nellie said, smiling. "That's why I love you."

"Besides, we can use his cell phone."

"Are we getting a little brother?" Toby asked.

"Looks like," Nellie said. "I just hope we can all finally change out of these clothes. And pee someplace where there's no poison ivy."

Each of them in turn ran into the store to clean up as best they could. Jac arrived, dazed, tent folded, ready to go, and they piled into the car. Herb was already gone. It seemed as though Sparkplug's funeral had been days ago. "Where to?" Nellie said, buckling in.

"The coast," said Todd.

"Good as any place," Nellie said. Then, *sotto voce* to Todd she added, "You and I have to talk."

"Big time," Todd said.

"Yeah, like, how does this end?" Anthony asked.

"TBD," said Todd.

Nellie steered toward the parking lot exit.

"Um, so, what exactly is 'this'?" Jac wanted to know.

"They're fugitives," Toby said excitedly.

"Is that all?" said Jac. "I mean, fine with me. I kicked a guy off a train."

"Did he die?" Anthony asked.

"I assume so," Jac said. "I mean, he didn't look too good before I kicked him off, so I kind of assume kicking him off sealed the deal."

"Was it going fast?" Toby asked. "The train?"

"Oh, yeah," said Jac. "O-o-oh, yeah."

There was a moment of silence.

"Nells," Todd said. "What is it?"

Now they saw that Nellie was crying.

"Nothing," she whispered.

"C'mon, Nellie," Toby said. "You just did a great thing. Seeing Herb through all that. That was amazing. You guys were great."

"Maybe," Nellie whimpered.

"Don't guess," Todd said. "You *know* you did good."

"But look how much bad I did!" Nellie insisted. The tires roared on the blacktop. No one knew what to say.

"Aw, Nells!" Todd said, placing his hand on her arm. "Maybe we did do some bad stuff. But in the end, look, you used your life for what a life should be used for. The people in that parking lot will never forget you. Society threw them away. You, like, retrieved them."

"Stop!" said Nellie. "I did a lot of bad, then we had this idea, and I didn't know I was going to end up wearing this thing so long. I didn't know people would want forgiveness from us. I didn't know what I was saying half the time. The only reason I did them any good was because I had to maintain my disguise. But I guess I helped some of them. Herb probably knew I was a fake, but he didn't care. I'm just gonna miss it, is all."

"We still have these costumes," Todd said brightly.

181

"No," Nellie sighed. "It's not the kind of thing you can pull off twice, costumes or not."

"Kinda thing that happens on the road," said Jac. "And you're right. It won't come again."

After a long time Nellie said, "Poor Sparkplug. I hope he's okay."

And then, silence.

The sun continued up and over, and, fueled by protein bars and bad coffee, they headed toward the coast. In Nebraska, herons migrated. In Colorado, the first snow swirled across the road. They stopped along the banks of the Great Salt Lake.

"First time I ever seen it," Jac mused.

"Same here," Todd said. "And maybe the last."

A great castle of mist loomed over them. Below, waves hissed and wind whipped sand at their faces. Four brown pelicans flapped low over the dunes. A freighter vanished into fog.

The three boys ran against the wind, up to the water's edge, pulled off their shoes, and rolled up their pants. Todd and Nellie huddled facing the dark purple-pink disc that shone through the mist. They wore their street clothes again. "At some point," Todd said, "someone has to turn their cell phone on for just a minute."

"Well, Jac—"

"No," Todd said. "One of us. We shouldn't really log onto personal accounts on his phone."

They heard the boys' laughter from the water's edge. "Do we sleep in the car tonight?" Nellie asked.

"We sleep a ways away," said Todd. "In the dunes. If the car is discovered—"

"Where do we go after here?" Nellie asked. "And what about them?"

Hoots rose from the trio cavorting in the surf.

"They can't answer for what we did," Todd said. "They get a new start." Nellie snuggled against him. He kissed the top of her head. "I just wanted to protect him," Todd said.

"I know," Nellie said.

The three came back, breathless. Todd watched Toby. Todd managed a smile. He tousled Toby's hair and kissed his cheek. "Me, too! Me, too!" Anthony cried. Todd gave him a kiss, too. And then Jac. Soon everyone had hugs and kisses from everyone else.

A few blocks inland they found a café with wooden tables and old-fashioned lamps and bad paintings. They ordered burgers and chili cheese fries and juice. Night came. They stayed with tea and the comfort of their own reflections.

When they could no longer look at crumbs on empty plates, they headed back to the beach. They pulled blankets out of the back of the car and headed for the dunes. There they tucked themselves into a hollow in the sand. Surf thundered. Out in the mist lights pulsed and vanished. The three boys spooned under their blanket. Todd and Nellie walked off into the maelstrom of wind, sand, and fog. "So where to?" she asked. "South? Out of the country?" She glanced back. "We can't take them."

"No." A wave broke like a gun going off.

"We just leave them here?"

"They'll find a way. There's trains and buses—"

"They can't call their parents."

"Or they could stay here."

"On their own?"

"It's been done. They've got each other. I bet Jac knows a trick or two."

"Legal or not."

"Look at the moon."

"Damn!"

"I love you, Nells. So much. You were the best nun ever!" He held her.

"I love you, too. Pretty damn good priest. And we'll figure this out. But it's for their own good we're cutting them loose. Isn't it?"

He nodded. "So when?"

"Soon."

"You don't want to let go of them any more than I do."

"I wasn't telling the whole truth when I said being a nun and listening to those people made me feel like a good person. I liked all this because I felt like a mom, too. I wonder if I'll ever have kids."

"I'd want you to have mine!"

"That's sweet!"

"It's true!"

They wandered out to where the surf bubbled and hissed at their feet. They held hands and watched the moon rise. "I can't sleep," Todd said.

"Want to make love?" Nellie asked.

Todd laughed. "Okay."

It was cold and damp and they were both anxious, but they managed, behind a dune far from the boys. They quickly dressed again, shivering and shuddering. "I still can't sleep," Todd said.

"Wanna check our phones?"

"Yeah."

"As briefly as possible."

"Can we answer messages?"

"No. The person we message would have to go to the police. We're fugitives, like Jac said. Your mom is out of her mind. You text her, she'll still be out of her mind." Nellie turned her phone on. "We just need to know if they're onto us."

The phone flashed logos and played electronic music, and the familiar icons flashed on. "Bunch of texts," Nellie said. She tapped the screen then cried, "Oh, my God!"

"What?"

"Littey got a search warrant for the bakehouse." She turned the phone off. "We're done. We're going now."

"What did he find?" Todd asked.

"Take your pick! How about blood matching three people who recently vanished?"

Todd pointed to where the boys slept. "Do we tell them?"

"We just go," Nellie said. "I can't deal with another goodbye. What if they begged us not to go?"

As they hustled to the car Todd glanced back. "What about money?" he said.

"Leave them half. There's an empty jar in the trunk. Put it in there. Go quick. Don't wake them."

They clicked the car open. Nellie got in. Todd retrieved the jar, counted out half their money, and stuffed it in.

"Hurry!" Nellie called after him. She waited, checking up and down the street. "Come on, come on!" she whispered to herself, shivering. Finally, Todd reappeared. The moonlight caught a tear on his cheek. He got in without a word.

A moment later, a single pair of headlights probed the empty street, paused, turned, and was gone. All fell silent but for the crash and seethe of surf.

In the dunes three young men slept, their dreams undisturbed.

As the car headed for the highway, Nellie finally spoke. "There is some good news," she said. "Mrs. Bishop texted me. Bammy Cetshwayo got into MIT on early decision."

Todd gave a thumbs up. A moment later, in a small voice, he sighed, "Never did get my muffin."

Nellie took his hand. "When we get where we're going," she said, "I'll buy you a *churro*."

Misty rays poked at the beach houses and cafés.

Toby woke and sat up. He looked around. Then he shook Anthony. "Hey!" he said.

185

Anthony jerked awake. "Huh?"

"Where are they?"

"I dunno. Were they here? Maybe they went for a walk."

Toby jumped to his feet and went this way and that. "Todd? Nellie?" Jac stirred.

"C'mon," Toby said. "We have to look for 'em."

"Gone," Jac said through a yawn.

"What, you saw?" Toby demanded. "You let 'em go?"

"Relax!" said Jac. "Fugitives never stay. I knew they'd go. But I didn't *know* know. Look. They left something."

Toby retrieved the jar. He cried even before opening it.

"Great," Jac said. "We can have breakfast. Pardon me if I think of, like, survival."

"No," Toby sighed. "I get it."

"I'm telling you," Jac said over breakfast, back at the same café, "it's a piece of cake. We can squat. Do something for a few bucks an hour. People think you can't do this stuff. You just put one foot after another."

Back outside Jac led them all in singing "This Train" at the tops of their voices as they walked into a neighborhood known for what he called "its vibrant street culture."

This meant a number of unshowered young people with backpacks and sometimes dogs or cats, wandering up and down or seated on curbs playing the guitar for change. Jac seemed to have a way with such folks, trading tales of trains ridden and cities seen.

By noon they had been offered to share space under a bridge in a nearby park, and someone thought they knew someone who needed "some lumber and stuff carried somewhere." That job never materialized, but a job sweeping out a Mexican restaurant did. Jac took that. Toby was hired by a record store. Anthony gave one of his under-the-bridge neighbors guitar lessons, and at night he stamped hands at an alt folk club. Eventually they

186

shared a room over the garage of a flaking Victorian home occupied by two women, seventeen cats, and a huge Hummel collection. Jac slept on a balcony in the back, "so you guys can have sex."

They turned their phones on again and found that Toby and Anthony were objects of an interstate manhunt, with both sets of parents pleading for "anything anyone knows."

"Yeah," Jac sneered. "If they'd only cared that much when you were there. Now they're weeping for the cameras. Huh! Let 'em try to find you!"

Toby and Anthony were afraid they were doing something illegal, but they loved being on their own, together. They didn't want it to end.

Sometimes in those weeks, when he was alone, Toby took out his phone and read and reread a text he had found when he had first turned it back on. It was date-stamped the morning Todd and Nellie had left, at 2:58 a.m.

"Dear Toby," it said, "Gotta make this quick because, well, you know. I love you Tobias. I am your truest, greatest friend ever, except Anthony obvs. I saw you grow to be a man and I wanted so much to help you and protect you. It's all I ever wanted. In the end I didn't do it the right way, and I can't explain now but just know that I'll always love you, Tobes, and I'll always be thinking of you. When you get back home visit my mom and sometimes visit my dad's grave, okay? He'll be expecting you. And when you guys have Tobias, Jr., I want you to love him and protect him the right way and don't mess up like me. XO to you, Anthony and Jac. See you sometime maybe. Nellie sends love, too. Love, Todd."

One day, as Toby read this for the twentieth time and wiped away tears, a woman's voice called from below. "Halloo-oo-oo!" Anthony and Jac were chopping wood down there, and Toby heard Anthony exclaim, "Oh, my God!" He hurried to the top of the stairs.

"Well, there you are!"

"Mrs. Bishop!" said Toby. "What—? How come—? How did you know we were here?"

"It's good to see you boys again," said Mrs. Bishop. She turned to Jac. "You must be Jac," she said.

"How did you know that?" Jac demanded.

"I have been a mathematics teacher for forty-one years," said Mrs. Bishop. "I know everything. And right now, I need one of those things that's a cup of coffee with an espresso in it—?"

"A red-eye," said Jac. "There's an awesome place on the next block."

"Then lead on!" said Mrs. Bishop.

They sat in the sun outside the awesome place. "This is Heaven," said Mrs. Bishop, sipping.

"You got the Sumatra, right?" said Jac.

"Aeropressed," said Mrs. Bishop. "At home I'm partial to Yirgacheffe, but I thought, I'm in a new place, I'll try something new!"

"Mrs. Bishop," said Toby. "You said when you got the coffee you'd tell us what's going on."

"Oh, yes. Well, I came to get you."

"What if we don't want to be gotten?" said Anthony.

"Yeah," Toby said. "This thing is kind of working out."

"More than 'kind of,'" said Jac.

"I see," said Mrs. Bishop, taking another sip.

"Are our parents behind this?" Anthony asked.

"Careful," said Mrs. Bishop. "May I point out that parents can be useful? Up to a point."

"Not mine," said Toby.

"Or mine," said Anthony.

"Well," Mrs. Bishop said, "let me tell you. When I ascertained where you were, you see, I went to your parents. To your *mothers*, separately. I told them I would retrieve you, if and only if they promised no more conversion camps. I told them that if they gave me any trouble I'd deny I knew anything. They thought the police could make me tell. I went all innocent and said, 'Well, I guess I don't know anything.' They wised up.

"Now, you two *will* be questioned. Needless to say there is a great brouhaha at home. But I don't know of any actual evidence tying you to, well, you'll find out to what."

"But I still don't get how you found us, how you *knew*," Toby insisted.

"I told you," Mrs. Bishop said slowly, "I have my ways, and I do not always tell what they are."

Toby and Anthony exchanged glances. "Okay," Anthony said. "Well, what happens now?"

"How about a walk on the beach?" Mrs. Bishop said. "Then I could really go for some Mexican!"

CHAPTER EIGHTEEN

An emotional homecoming—Moving scenes of
familial affection, &c.—Strange news from abroad—
Jac's decision—Eastward, ho!

The reader can only imagine the tears, accusations, embraces, recriminations, warnings, kisses, and promises when Mrs. Bishop brought Toby and Anthony home. She also brought Jac, who, though uncertain about settling down, agreed to come along and be a distraction from all the parental hand-wringing and scolding and pleading and preaching, to say nothing of police interrogations and national and local TV at everyone's doorsteps. Mrs. Bishop agreed to take Jac in, for the time being.

Life was not simple for Toby or Anthony. Toby insisted to the police that he knew nothing about Nellie's bakehouse, even though Nellie's parents reported that he had come by just before she and Todd disappeared. Toby admitted that Nellie and Todd had impersonated religious personnel, but Anthony swore Bates had freely released him from the Bending Sheep. No fingerprints were found on Bates's gun but his own, but there was a fresh round of interrogations about his suicide. Warrants for Nellie and Todd remained in place, but finally the police had exhausted every last bit Toby and Anthony might know, and at last they left them alone. The camera crews moved on, and Mrs. Bishop wisely advised that everyone decline financial offers for their stories of how they had known the young man CNN called "The Fiend of Fleet High."

Though they had marked Mrs. Bishop's warning about any more conversion camps, Toby's and Anthony's parents still preached antigay sentiments at home and would not let the two see each other.

But they could not make this work perfectly. Both boys drove. Keeping them tucked at home became difficult, especially with Mrs. Bishop going out of her way to greet their mothers in church or the supermarket, making discreet remarks about the oppression she had heard went on at their homes. More than once she invited the boys over, then suddenly remembered that she "had to go out for a couple of hours."

One afternoon, a few weeks after their return, Mrs. Bishop asked all three young men to have a more serious talk. "Have you seen the papers?" she asked quietly as she motioned for them to sit in her parlor.

"There has been an accident," she said, reaching for their hands.

Toby's lip trembled. Anthony enveloped him in a hug.

"In Mexico," Mrs. Bishop continued. "A car of the right description. Everything was badly burned. And everyone."

Toby sobbed. Anthony held him and rocked him, repeating, "Oh, my baby!"

"However," Mrs. Bishop continued with a sigh, "the vehicle's occupants remain unknown. The license plate was missing. The bodies were unrecognizable, and the Mexican government refuses to release them until the United States promises not to build the wall."

"That's crazy!" Anthony exclaimed.

"Crazy or not," Mrs. Bishop said, "there it is. It's probably against international law. It's probably against a lot of things. But the bodies are south of the border, and that's where they're going to stay. All we know is the make and model of the car, and it does fit."

"What about a registration?" Anthony demanded. Toby's body just shook.

"Burned," said Mrs. Bishop. "The car turned over, exploded, and burned all night. It was in a very remote area."

That night Toby reread Todd's final communication to him. When he read the words "See you sometime maybe," his eyes flooded so he could not go on. Then he thought how, someday, he and Anthony might have a son. And that son would grow up and finally leave for college, and Toby would say to him, "See you sometime, maybe." And Toby thought how, if there had been some terrible mistake about the car accident and Todd did see him again, they would both be different. Nights cuddled in the comfort of boyish bedrooms were over. It was time for Toby to protect and defend himself. And Anthony and Jac and Mrs. Bishop and whoever else needed it.

The next evening Toby went to the cemetery. Mrs. Sweeney had refused to put up a stone for Todd until his death was officially confirmed. In the meantime, Toby had been visiting that one small, familiar stone at the back. "Hey, Mr. Sweeney," he said, when he got there that evening. "It's me, your second son. I guess maybe your first son is with you now. We don't know. But whatever happened, I thought I should come say 'Hi' to you. You were always an inspiration to me. And, well, I was just wondering if I could say something to you. Something I guess maybe you know, that I could never say to my own dad, not even now. But you're my second dad, and I know you'll understand, so here goes." Toby cleared his throat. "Dad, I have something to tell you. I'm gay. I like other men, and I have a very special man I love, Anthony. And he loves me, and I want to be with him for the rest of my life. So congratulations. You've got a third son. Maybe you'll have grandkids! Oh, and Mrs. Sweeney has been real super nice to us. I see why you love her so much. So, that's all. I'll see you soon again, sir. Thanks for listening."

Mrs. Bishop offered to adopt Jac, if he could emancipate himself. At first he refused. "I belong on the road," he said. "I appreciate all you did for me, Mrs. B., but I'm a rambling man." Mrs. Bishop countered with arguments about education and "making a solid start in life," and Jac would say, "I already started, a long time ago."

But Mrs. Bishop noticed that Jac would suddenly, casually announce longish-term plans, especially regarding their coffee supply. "And when this is gone," he said of their just-bought Blue Mountain, "we'll try the Maragogipe." He pressed Mrs. Bishop for a siphon coffee maker. "Grosche Heisenberg GR 285," he insisted, as they strolled through a Labor Day sale at a nearby mall.

"Those things look like science experiments," Mrs. Bishop objected. "And they cost too much."

"Get it for me for Christmas!" Jac exclaimed, then clapped his hand over his mouth.

"You planning on staying?"

Jac waited a bit to say, "Maybe."

"In the car you talked about trying out for the musical at school. That would take you up to Thanksgiving. Then you'd *have* to finish the semester, wouldn't you?"

A couple of nights later Jac casually mentioned to Mrs. Bishop that he had researched "emancipation" and its requirements in their state.

Jac was a hit playing Cinderella's Prince in *Into the Woods*, and that Christmas morning, with his paperwork well advanced, he opened a brand new Grosche Heisenberg GR 285 coffee siphon and a bag of kopi luwak. By spring, he was Jac Bishop.

❖ ❖ ❖

Toby and Anthony were so distracted by their families and their studies that they could not spend as much time as they would have liked with the most pitiable figure in our story—Mrs. Sweeney. Bereft of husband and son, she spent her days wondering where she had gone wrong and fretting that what CNN had said was true. Even when the police were convinced of her personal innocence, she was harassed by the occasional rock thrown through a window, or by self-styled young rebels who sought her autograph because they thought what her son had done was "awesomely insurgent." One young woman declared herself a "high priestess in the Church of Todd," and Officer Littey had to forcibly remove her, her sleeping bag, and several scented candles from Mrs. Sweeney's porch.

When, in addition to these troubles, she mentioned to Jac that she drank Folger's, she suddenly had a new friend. Every time he came by he found a new way to tell her that, in the few hours he'd known her son, he had found him special and had been inspired by him. He told her how Todd had played the part of Sister Richardine, and then "a priest who I think we forgot to name!" They laughed, though Mrs. Sweeney never quite understood the story or why Jac insisted that she never repeat it. "Well," she would conclude. "I don't know about all that, but I do know we should have another one of those Kona pour-overs!"

Jac told people that, "professionally," his name was now "Jac Bishop-Sweeney."

"What profession?" Toby asked. "You're a barista."

"Don't be a dick," Jac said. "I am a future small-business owner."

If Jac had confused Mrs. Sweeney, one can only imagine she became even more confused the next Thanksgiving when Herb rolled up with his new dog, a peppy female

195

beagle named Quadrant, and showered adoration on "the woman who raised that fine young priest."

Later, with tears in his eyes, Herb told the boys, "I never did hear from anyone who found Sparkplug. I just hope he's okay."

Years passed and all the boys went to college. Jac had to be dragged kicking and screaming, but Anthony convinced him that he needed a business degree to fulfill his dreams as a purveyor of coffees and teas.

Far away, Bamedele Cetshwayo also studied hard, and when it came time for him to graduate from MIT, his parents offered to fly Mrs. Bishop and a guest to the commencement ceremony.

She of course chose her son, then paid for Toby and Anthony, too. That morning the car came while it was still dark. Jac filled thermal mugs with a new "graduation blend" he had created from coffees grown near Bammy's birthplace.

First light grew at the end of the highway. The sky was overcast. Anthony sipped coffee and checked Facebook. "Herb and Quadrant are in Virginia," he said. "They saw the wild horses. And we have to give the priest's mom a big hug!" Then silently he searched on Facebook, as he often did, for Joshua, and once again, he did not find him.

He then scrolled through some HuffPo headlines. "Oh, thank God!" he said.

"For what?" said Jac.

"You know that awful conservative mayor in the north of England?"

They all groaned.

"He's been missing for two weeks. They just declared there'll be a new election, and the favorite is a Muslim woman."

"That should turn things around," said Mrs. Bishop. "Are they sure he's really gone?"

"Now that the election has been announced," Anthony said, "they have to go with it. He's out."

"Where does someone like that disappear to?" Toby wondered.

"And it's a good thing," Anthony continued, "because it says otherwise that city is doing really well. Bars, restaurants, tourists, new stadium, everything."

The car hummed along down the highway.

"Completely redid the waterfront," Anthony said, scrolling. "Took this old warehouse and made a food court. Organic artisanal everything." The car hummed. "Huh! They even had a pop-up pie shop!"

"A pop-up pie shop?" Toby asked.

"Yeah," said Anthony. "Apparently it was real popular."

"Wow," said Toby.

"Run by some weird offshoot of the Catholic Church," Anthony added. "Then it disappeared. Everyone's hoping it'll return."

"Maybe it will," Toby said, brushing away a tear and looking out the window.

"Maybe it will," Mrs. Bishop echoed.

Rain streaked the windows. Jac had never been in a plane so he held Mrs. Bishop's hand. Toby and Anthony held hands with each other as they all crept across the tarmac. Then they stopped. Then moved forward. Then the plane began to roar and shudder and go fast. "What's happening?" Jac demanded. Mrs. Bishop smiled at him. "My son," she said, and kissed his forehead. The plane roared and raced and soon there was nothing under them and the home they knew grew small below.

Clouds enveloped them. The cabin rocked suddenly and everybody held tighter to each other. Then the shaking stopped, the clouds fell away, and a golden morning filled the cabin.

Toby looked out and smiled to think of them, Todd and Nellie, wearing ridiculous disguises and merrily selling empanadas. He thought of all the mornings he woke with Todd, from when they were five or six up until just— Well, he guessed now that it had been a while. He thought of the morning he and Anthony and Jac woke on the beach. How he cried but how they all went and found friends and a home and jobs. Now, all of them would graduate and would at last discover who they really were and what they would really do.

He looked out. The plane banked and light flashed off the wing—like a loving wink from a friend. He smiled. To the tilting wing he said, "Hey. See you sometime."

Next to him, Mrs. Bishop chuckled and said, "A pop-up pie shop. Imagine that!"

ACKNOWLEDGMENTS

Without the following people, *Todd Sweeney* would not have been what it is. So, here is who to blame, in alphabetical order:

Lou Ceci, for his meticulous advice.

John Corser, for being a most adaptable Todd.

Jameson Currier, for yet more meticulous advice.

Ann McMan, for cheerleading and a great design sense.

Rogério Pinto, for reading with a fine sensibility and for offering the most loving encouragement to my baser tendencies.

Kelly Smith, for a fine eye and fine taste in creating the book's interior.

Jane Lincoln Taylor, a great editor and proofreader who let all the naughty bits stand.

Toni Whitaker, for creating the ebook.

Nicholas Williams, for a stunning cover and a good-natured willingness to take on all related jobs, with little warning and with way too much supervision.

ABOUT THE AUTHOR

DAVID PRATT is the author of the novels *Bob the Book* (Lambda Literary Award winner), *Wallaçonia,* and *Looking After Joey.* He has published many pieces of short fiction, some of which are collected in *My Movie.* David has performed his work for the stage in various venues in New York City and Detroit. He lives in Michigan.

WALLAÇONIA

a novel
DAVID PRATT

"The voyage of a boy who wins his own sense of manhood. A wonderfully written, original coming-of-age tale."

—*Lambda Literary Review*

"Sharp. Focused. Super-intense, and special. It's rare to find a novel with such a beautifully rendered friendship between a young gay man and an older mentor."

—Bill Konigsburg, author of *Openly Straight* and *The Porcupine of Truth*

Wallaçonia cover photo by Dot

Beautiful Dreamer Press

www.BeautifulDreamerPress.com